# LIFELESS IN THE LIBRARY

## A MOORECLIFF MANOR CAT COZY MYSTERY BOOK 4

### LEIGHANN DOBBS

The fifth annual Moorecliff Manor Cat Show, a yearly event held to raise money for the local animal shelter, was to take place in the Moorecliffs' luxurious black-and-cream-themed formal ballroom. The participants, who would be staying at Moorecliff Manor for the duration of the show, had already arrived.

Today, Araminta Moorecliff was dressed in her finest magenta-and-yellow outfit as she stood surveying the ballroom where the competition's participants were readying things at their respective stations.

Nina Bellaforte was in attendance with her Russian Blue, Zsa Zsa.

In her early forties, Nina was a clearly bleached blonde, and from the designer outfits she'd been wearing since she arrived at the manor, Araminta guessed she was a woman of expensive tastes as well.

Millicent Copperfield, a dark-haired, middle-aged,

youthful-looking woman with voluminous dark hair, a slim figure, and lots of mascara, was there with her cat, Jasmine—a pure-white Persian. The two were accompanied by Millicent's husband, Donald.

Araminta realized two things about Donald the moment the couple had arrived. Donald was henpecked. He did everything his wife told him, agreed with everything she said. Araminta found it a bit odd. It seemed Donald was wealthy, and in such circumstances, the groveling usually occurred the other way around. More like *always* when the motivator was money. The other thing she noticed was that perhaps Donald was going through a bit of a midlife crisis or something because it was clear he dyed his hair—probably to hide the gray. She supposed he wasn't ready for the world to know he was becoming an "older man."

Stephen Roy was a skinny little guy, soft-spoken, and nervous. His large Norwegian Forest cat, Bjorn, was in the competition. Araminta wasn't very fond of the guy for reasons she wasn't yet sure of, but she certainly loved his cat.

This morning, he was arguing with someone who seemed oddly familiar, but she couldn't quite place the woman because she was at the far side of the ballroom, partially hidden by a large potted plant, and… well… Araminta hated to admit it, but at that distance, things were a bit blurry. It probably didn't help that she'd skipped her last vision appointment. Maybe, like Harold —the Moorecliffs' butler—she had finally reached an age where she needed glasses?

All this cat watching turned Araminta's thoughts to her own felines, Sasha and Arun, a pair of gorgeous Siamese cats. They weren't in the contest, as it wouldn't be fair for her to enter her own cats, though their absence didn't mean that her outfit was absent of cat hair. She plucked a few hairs, creamy white with a chocolaty-brown tip, off her outfit and scanned the room for the cats. She hadn't seen them in hours. Perhaps they were hiding in the attic to avoid the commotion, though it was more likely they were skulking around, planning some sort of shenanigans.

Trinity, the Moorecliffs' maid, walked up beside her, and Araminta took advantage of the younger woman's eyesight. "That one seems oddly familiar, Trin. Can you tell who it is?"

"That's Vivianne Underwood, remember? She's the one you saved from going to prison for Joey Tuccinelli's murder a few weeks ago."

"How interesting. She was just arguing with Stephen a moment ago. Hmm. I wonder why?"

Trinity shrugged. "He's Viv's new boyfriend, apparently. Did you know she took over collections for the organization now that Tony's in jail?"

Araminta didn't know, but it made sense now why Stephen seemed so nervous. The "organization" wasn't exactly one that was a pillar of society. In fact, it involved a bit of organized crime mixed in with seedy legitimate enterprises. Having an argument with the person who was responsible for collecting money owed couldn't be good for one's health.

The head of the organization, Tony "the Fist" Romano, was currently spending his days in prison, but his cronies were still out there, doing his dirty work for him—and according to Trinity, that included Vivianne. Did Stephen owe Tony Romano money? Was that why he'd entered Bjorn in this competition?

"Ahh. Perhaps that's why he's here. He needs to win the competition because he owes the organization money."

"Could be." Trinity shrugged again. "I wouldn't know. Since things quieted down after Joey's murder was resolved, Viv doesn't talk to me as much."

Araminta hugged the younger woman. "Don't worry, Trin. Viv may have taken her life in a new direction, one that doesn't involve old friendships so much, but we Moorecliffs couldn't live without you. We still want you around."

Trinity thanked her then motioned to the only other man who had entered a cat in the competition. "Who is that?"

"Clint Sterling. Foster Sterling's son."

Trinity's mouth made an O, and Araminta nodded. "Yep, one and the same!"

Clint Sterling had entered his exotic Bengal, Loughley, this year, but it wasn't as if he were here for the prize money. No, rather, his father was a well-known cat fancier, and he needed to make a good showing in this competition, or his father's opinion of him would turn less than enthusiastic.

The Bengal was a new breed, some sort of mix with

a leopard or something. Araminta had to admit the cat was striking, but it reminded her of a coat she'd once had with the distinctive black circular markings.

"It looks like everyone is almost ready. I better get back to the dusting!"

Araminta waved her off and went back to perusing this year's entrants and their owners who'd come for the competition. Her features relaxed when her gaze fell on Daphne Burgess. She was a longtime friend of both Jacob Hershey, who was personally attending the show for the first time since Araminta had begun the annual competition five years ago, and of Araminta herself. Daphne had a very large Maine Coon named Shaggy, who was also in this year's show.

Jacob was also in attendance, though Araminta had no idea where he was at the moment. He'd arrived last night with his fluffy black-and-gray cat, Codger. At first, Araminta had thought he intended to ask for a late entry for the cat, but Jacob assured her that Codger was much too persnickety to participate in a cat show.

Araminta hoped that she, Jacob, and Daphne would get to catch up at some point during the competition. It had been a while since they'd had a chance to talk, and Araminta was sure there were lots of things they could talk about.

Harold joined her at the entrance to the ballroom, a frown pulling at his features.

"Something wrong, Harold?"

"Not yet, but there's plenty of time, and from what

I've overheard with these new hearing aids of mine, it could be disastrous."

Araminta didn't like the worry in his tone or the word he'd chosen. She had hopes of an enjoyable show with a group of lovely folks and their cats, who were even lovelier. "What did you hear?"

His brows rose. "Too much, if you don't mind my saying so, but the last bit was more worrisome than most, given the past months' events here at the manor. A woman said she'd only give up in this competition 'over her dead body.' Given the number of bodies we've been shocked by or stumbled over lately… murder at the manor seems to have become a pattern."

Araminta hurried to reassure him. "I know we've been through a lot, Harold, but this is a cat show, not a showdown between humans. Trust me, you have nothing to worry about."

The words had barely left her lips before a blood-curdling shriek split the air.

# CHAPTER TWO

*A*ll eyes turned in the direction of the shriek—Millicent's station. She had Jasmine in her arms and a horrified expression on her face. Was something wrong with her prized kitty? Oh no. Araminta rushed over to her table to find out what was going on.

Araminta winced. In Jasmine's lovely white fur was a big, ugly, hair-matted glob of pink. Millicent screeched again, then the babble of hysteria started. "Oh, my poor dear. Matted and tangled, and look! Look what I found, all mushed in her fur. Gum! And the show is about to start—I don't have time for attempting the peanut butter remedy, even if it were available." She slammed the grooming comb onto the table. "Someone is going to pay for this."

Cuddling the cat close, Millicent crooned apologies to her cat. As she did so, Jasmine curled her fluffy tail up into Millicent's face, creating a spectacle that made Millicent appear to have a thick, white mustache.

Behind Araminta, there was a bit of a snort before Nina spoke. "Oh my. That's going to be difficult to remove."

Her words seemed sympathetic, but her tone? Not so much. Araminta turned to ask if she'd seen anyone near Jasmine's carrier who might have put the gum in Jasmine's fur. The same instant, she saw the big pink bubble. Nina drew the gum back into her mouth, and it made a big pop, right before she smiled at Millicent and walked away.

"I'll ask Trinity to bring up some peanut butter and ice," Araminta offered, but Millicent shook her head.

"There's no time. The judges are already here."

It was true. All four judges had arrived in the ballroom and were speaking quietly to one another while the cat owners worked to ready their pets. The next hour was a bustle of prep. At every station, pet owners were grooming their cats to perfection, checking their nails, their ears, their fur... everything.

It was during this prep time that Araminta noticed that Nina and Donald, Millicent's husband, had paired off and were whispering furiously in the corner of the ballroom. Were they arguing about what had happened to Jasmine? For a moment, she wished she had Harold's hearing aids because she would love to hear what the two of them were saying.

Araminta glanced over her shoulder at Millicent. Trinity had brought peanut butter and ice from the kitchen, but it looked like Millie had decided there was nothing to be done other than quick, complete removal of the sticky wad of pink gum from Jasmine's fur. Scissors had been brought to the table, and both Millicent and Trinity had heads down, carefully snipping the gum from Jasmine's otherwise luxurious coat.

Unusually loud female laughter drew Araminta's attention from Millicent and Trinity to Nina. She'd left her conversation with Don and was now leaning on the low table that had been set up for Clint Sterling. She was smiling and obviously flirting with the man, but Clint, bless his dedicated heart, was hardly paying her sultry overtures a bit of attention.

Finally, the judging was underway. The cats were examined, poked, and prodded. The judges hmmed and scribbled notes on their clipboards while the owners of each cat filled his or her ears with information particular to their specific breed.

Stephen, Araminta noticed, was being particularly bold with his time before the judges—she could hear his attempts to make the judges take note of how his cat, Bjorn, had a longer, fluffier, and therefore nicer tail than Zsa Zsa—the Russian Blue they'd seen at the previous station. Zsa Zsa had a much shorter, stumpier one, he informed them, and all the while, his eyes darted from the judges to Nina and back again.

*So fidgety*, Araminta thought. Although he attempted to hide the fact, she could clearly see the man was nervous. He was going overboard pointing out Bjorn's strong points.

In the end, the contestants were surprised by the feline who took the round. Previously, everyone had expected Jasmine to win. She did not, and Araminta was sure she knew why. Unfortunately, Millicent had made the call to cut the gum from her cat's fur, and even with the expert guidance of Trinity, who had experience with cutting and styling human hair, her pet's lovely white Persian coat was not the same.

Loughley, Clint Sterling's exotic Bengal, took the first round.

"Well, that certainly seems to have shaken things up a little," Jacob told Araminta. He'd come in during the final moments, when the contestants did their routine holding of their breaths, before the judges announced their decisions.

Daphne joined them. "He's new to the circuit, you know."

Araminta nodded. "But prepared and thorough. It's clear he really wants to win this thing."

"Hmm." Daphne nodded. "He does have that look of determination in his eyes. I, personally, find it a bit harsh. I mean, it seems to go beyond general determination, you know? Yes, I know who his father is and that Clint really wants to impress him, but I get the feeling he's the kind of guy who will do whatever it takes to win this competition."

Araminta wasn't sure she agreed with Daphne's assessment, but her words struck a chord somewhere in the region of her gut, and suddenly, this year's competition took on an ominous feel.

# CHAPTER THREE

"*I* personally wouldn't want to be poked, prodded, and trotted about just to win a stupid contest." Codger lay atop the stone wall under a fig tree in the Moorecliff Manor atrium. He was leisurely grooming his front paw as the sun warmed his fluffy black-and-gray fur.

The cats had decided to convene in the atrium because it was the perfect place to watch the comings and goings in the house. It was situated in the middle of the U-shaped structure of Moorecliff Manor and therefore protected on three sides by the house with a gate on the fourth side.

From their vantage point, they could gaze into several sets of French doors that led to various parts of the mansion—the solarium, a grand hallway where the library was, and, of course, the ballroom, where the judging for the cat show was now taking place.

The atrium was a favorite of Arun and Sasha as it

afforded all the protection of being indoors with all the excitement of being outdoors. Here, they could lounge about under a variety of trees, shrubs, and flowers where delicious-looking birds flitted on the branches above and chipmunks provided a sporting chase when the cats were so inclined.

Arun gazed into the ballroom and shuddered at the thought of being judged. "I agree wholeheartedly."

"I don't know. A blue ribbon would be kind of nice." Sasha's voice was soft.

Arun was surprised to see a hint of longing in her sky-blue eyes. Did she desire to win a silly contest? Arun couldn't fathom it himself, but who could understand what women wanted?

"I'm sure you would be a shoo-in to win with your luxurious, silky, cream-colored coat and velvety-brown markings." Arun looked in toward the ballroom, where the judge was placing a blue ribbon on the Bengal cat. "I see that Loughley has taken the first round. He seems a bit stuck up. What do you make of him?"

"Odd duck," Codger said in his usual blunt manner. "His markings are very nice though."

The Bengal was sitting up proudly, displaying the circular markings on his side. They were nearly perfect in size and symmetry. "Yeah, I see what you mean. I just hope things go well. Araminta has put her heart and soul into this contest."

Codger grunted. "At least they aren't killing each other to win. That might cause our respective owners to enter into their usual investigatory contest to see who can solve it first."

Araminta and Jacob had a competitive streak when it came to solving mysteries. It had been going on their entire lives since they were young, and Jacob was on the police force himself. Of course, now they were older and retired, but that didn't stop them from trying to solve the unusual amount of murders that seemed to happen at Moorecliff Manor.

"True, but it seems they have been getting along a little better lately. Their typically antagonistic competitions have taken on a more friendly tone." Sasha preened her long white whiskers.

"There may have not been a murder, but some of the contestants *are* acting a little suspicious," Arun said.

"Have you checked their rooms?" Codger asked.

"Of course. I snuck in when Trinity was vacuuming. I haven't found too much unusual except for maybe the Copperfields' room," Arun said.

"Oh?" Codger raised his bushy brows.

"It appears they have a suite, and one of them is sleeping on the couch."

"A troubled marriage?" Sasha asked.

"Perhaps. Donald is trying to act younger. He has all sorts of skin and hair elixirs," Arun said.

"I noticed he dyes his fur," Codger said. "Jacob tried that once. Made a mess all over the house, and the smell was quite nasty." Codger turned his nose up.

"It does smell rather noxious, doesn't it?" Sasha

wrinkled her dainty nose. "But I didn't smell that sort of scent in the Copperfields' room."

Arun nodded. "Thankfully, he only has face creams and pomades. The smell is not so strong on those."

"There's another person who is up to something." Sasha batted at a leaf with her paw.

"Who?" Codger asked.

"Nina Bellaforte. She had someone in her room last night. I heard her giggling when I walked past on my way for a midnight snack."

"What?" Codger seem surprised and maybe a bit impressed with Sasha's powers of observation. "Right under everyone's noses?"

"Bold, isn't it? But I don't think she is a very nice person." Sasha turned to look into the ballroom. "Oh, they are starting to pack everything up."

Arun swiveled his attention toward the dining room. "Trinity is setting the plates out on the table."

"The guests that are staying at the Manor will soon retire to the dining room for dinner." Sasha stood and stretched her front paws out in front of her. "I say we hurry in and get in position under the tablecloth before anyone notices so that we can take advantage of any morsels that may fall to the floor."

# CHAPTER FOUR

The next morning, preparation for the second round of judging started early. The competitors had risen before the sun to have breakfast so they'd have plenty of time to prepare. They were now making their way to the ballroom to begin the day by readying their pets for the upcoming activities.

In the background, Araminta could hear Daisy and Harold cheerfully welcoming attendees. The sound of Daisy's chipper voice brought a smile to her face. She'd grown very close to her niece-in-law after the untimely death of her nephew, Archie.

Daisy had proven to be a woman of great character and a big heart despite the fact that some in the family had thought she was a gold digger only after the Moorecliff money. As Araminta had always known, Daisy was nothing of the sort despite her being much younger than Archie. Archie had always loved hosting the cat show, and Daisy had eagerly agreed to continue the tradition.

It was barely eight o'clock, and already, the manor was bustling with movement and sound. Everything was as it should be... or so it seemed. All night, she had been unable to shake the uneasiness she'd felt after Daphne's comments. But so far, nothing untoward had occurred, so she headed to the ballroom to check on the cats and their owners and to make sure all was well at each of their stations.

"Good morning, Araminta. Headed to the ballroom?" Jacob asked. He'd just come downstairs from one of the guest rooms on the second floor, and she couldn't help but notice he looked particularly dapper this morning.

Codger was following along at his heels, and Sasha and Arun, who had been walking alongside Araminta, darted over to greet him.

"Yes, I was. Would you care to join me?" she offered, then, "Good morning to yourself, as well, Codger. Are you enjoying your stay?"

Jacob laughed. "I do believe he spent the night with Sasha and Arun in the upstairs foyer, trying to decide which of the competing cats would be worthy of his company."

He joined her near the bottom of the stairs, and out of old habit ingrained years ago, Araminta looped her arm through his.

"Agility today," she reminded him. It was to be the competition's second phase.

"Oh, I know, I know," he told her, following his words with a chuckle. "I will admit I'm quite looking forward to it."

Today, the judges would be particularly interested in each of the competing felines' particular agilities. Araminta always enjoyed this stage of the competition, as cats—being a rather bossy and most times finicky lot—didn't always like to do as they were told. This portion of the show, more than any other, would keep the audience smiling. As owners urged their kitties through each phase of the agility contest and their cats decided whether or not to go along, there were always plenty of comical moments.

"Myself as well," she told Jacob. "I suspect we will get quite a few laughs, especially from Jasmine and Bjorn."

During the walk to the ballroom, Araminta listened with half an ear while Jacob talked about catching up with Daphne while he was here for the cat show, but her thoughts were racing ahead to the morning activities. It was early, but she knew they would find what she'd often referred to as "controlled chaos" in the ballroom. Groomers attending their charges, veterinarians making sure all was well with the cats before the show. Local newspeople trying to get sound bites. Once these people finished their morning check-ins, the owners would take over, brushing and fluffing their cats, making sure everything was as perfect as it could be before the judges arrived.

The first thing she noticed when she and Jacob

stepped through the large double doors was that Zsa Zsa was still in her crate. The poor dear. She didn't seem at all interested in what was going on around her. In fact, she looked bored, with her round golden eyes half slitted, but… why wasn't Nina grooming her, as the other contestants' owners were doing with their cats?

"One moment, Jacob," she said, excusing herself while extracting her arm from his. Jacob nodded and promised to see her later, to which Araminta absently waved him off. "I hope you enjoy the show."

Jacob had barely gone ten feet before Araminta started her visual search of the room for Nina. She was nowhere. Perhaps she'd gone to the bathroom?

Sure that was the reason for her absence, Araminta walked over to Zsa Zsa's crate and bent down to croon a human-to-cat good morning. Sasha and Arun inserted themselves between her and the crate, making it practically impossible for her to get close enough to pet the kitty through the crate door.

Admonishing her loves for their jealousy, Araminta picked up Sasha and headed to the next station to ask about Nina but drew up sharply, her gaze flying to the ballroom doors when a horrified shriek echoed through the hallways and filtered into the ballroom. The shriek had come from somewhere far within the manor, and there was such a hubbub going on in the room that it could barely be heard over the noise of activity.

Araminta instantly recognized the voice as Trinity's, and her heart leapt into her throat. Had something happened to her or Mary or Harold or Yancy or, God forbid, one of the members of the Moorecliff family?

Sasha leapt from her arms and raced to the doors, Arun keeping step beside her.

Harold met her outside the ballroom doors and caught her arm before she could head toward the solarium.

"It came from the library, ma'am," he said, turning her in that direction.

Araminta couldn't help but be grateful his hearing aids had finally arrived. "Thank you, Harold."

He nodded but then paused. "I'll have to leave you here, Araminta. I'm afraid I just heard someone approaching the door."

Araminta nodded and hurried toward the library, marveling at how well Harold's hearing aids worked if he could hear someone approach the door. Must drive him crazy though. Maybe he should turn them down just a tad.

As family estate houses went, Moorecliff Manor was by no means small, which meant it was no short distance from the ballroom to the library. Araminta arrived to discover that Daisy, Mary the cook, and Stephanie, Araminta's grandniece, were already there. Weariness etched each of their faces. Daisy had her arms around a sobbing Trinity, obviously trying to calm the girl.

"What on earth has happened?" Araminta asked. She had to admit she was relieved to see her little family all well and accounted for. For a minute there, she'd been afraid that there had been another body.

But seeing as the summer had been full of bodies at Moorecliff Manor, Araminta was sure the odds were against another one popping up… until Daisy motioned to her left, and Araminta craned her neck to see feet sticking out from behind the desk.

"No! It can't be another one!" Araminta sidled into the room to get a better look.

Daisy nodded. "It's Mrs. Bellaforte, Minta. Trinity came in to clean up and found her there, on the floor. I'm afraid she is quite dead."

Arun rushed between Araminta's legs and darted behind the desk, Sasha close on his heels. Nina Bellaforte lay staring at the ceiling with sightless eyes. A purple bruise encircled her neck.

"She's been strangled!" Arun whispered.

"I can see that, and so can Araminta." Sasha angled her head upward to where Araminta was peering down at the crime scene.

"Good. Let's hope Jacob doesn't come upon us. This way, Araminta can get all the details first." Arun walked slowly around the corpse, taking in every detail.

"Why are these here?" Sasha stuck out her paw and touched a rose petal that lay on the floor. There were several of them, in fact, all around the body.

"Someone gave her a rose?" Arun looked around,

crouching close to the ground and scanning the surface for the rose stem. As a cat, he had the advantage of being able to get very close to floor level and, thus, find small things that humans sometimes missed.

"And why the book?" Sasha nodded toward the cat breed book that lay open on the floor.

"Perhaps she pulled it down in the struggle?" Arun glanced up at the rows of books, which appeared undisturbed. If she'd grabbed one during the struggle, would more books have come down? Or had she been reading it?

"If only I'd seen who she had in her room," Sasha said.

"You think that person is the killer?" Arun eyed the rose petals.

"Perhaps. But she was giggling, so it sounded as if they were on good terms."

"Things can turn bad quickly, especially if they were sneaking around."

"Indeed. But I think there is more going on. What about what we saw in the bathroom?"

Sasha looked up, her blue eyes wide. "Do you think that has something to do with the murder?"

"Perhaps. It's something out of the ordinary, and everything out of the ordinary needs to be investigated."

"True," Sasha agreed. "Then we must call it to Araminta's attention."

"Shoo… shoo…" Araminta waved at them. "Don't disturb the crime scene, you two!"

Arun flicked his tail. "Surely Araminta knows that we know better than to disturb the scene."

"But she does have a point. We should take our leave. I hear the police coming down the hallway." Sasha headed for the door.

"I'm right behind you. We've seen all we need to see anyway."

# CHAPTER FIVE

Daisy had called the police as soon as they'd made the grim discovery, and, in fact, it had been Detective Ivan Hershey and his team who Harold had heard at the door when he was escorting Araminta to the library. They'd arrived rather quickly, Araminta thought, almost as if they'd been lurking outside, just waiting for another murder to occur.

If it had been only Ivan, she might have thought he was lurking around, trying to catch a glimpse of Stephanie. The young detective and the girl had developed a fondness for each other, which Araminta thought was sweet. Never mind that Ivan was Jacob's grandson and probably just as stubborn as the old coot. Perhaps Araminta should warn Steph about that.

All of the cat show's competitors and their staff had been separated into various rooms in the manor as the police took statements.

Araminta was waiting in the parlor with the rest of

the Moorecliff family for the police to finish before any of her questions could be answered. Truth be told, she would probably have ducked her head in shame over having another murder connected to the Moorecliff family in any way, but she was too busy worrying about Trinity—the poor girl was beside herself, having been the one to find the body—and with trying to sort the facts in her head to think about the family's reputation.

She hadn't seen Jacob but knew that by now, he would have started his own investigation. He was probably trying to interrogate people in the ballroom before Ivan could stop him. Araminta smiled at the thought. With her and Jacob on the case, she was certain the killer would be brought to justice soon.

Detective Hershey approached, his expression dour. "If I believed in such things, I would declare either the Moorecliff family or the manor to be cursed."

"Oh, pooh, Detective. We both know better than that." Araminta waved away the nonsense. "Have your men found anything?"

He braced his feet apart and folded his hands behind his back then nodded. "Murder weapon. Rose petals at the crime scene but no roses in the room. A book on cat breeds near the body, but you were holding a cat show, so that one is no surprise."

"Except that it is," Araminta told him. "Nina knew cats. Why would she be looking at a book about breeds?"

Detective Hershey peered at her. "Why would there be rose petals? A lovers' quarrel?"

*More like a competitor quarrel,* Araminta thought. She remembered the gum in Jasmine's fur. Nina had been chewing gum, and nobody doubted she'd put the pink mess in the cat's fur to cause problems for Millicent in the first stage of the show. But Araminta didn't believe Millicent was so enraged she would kill over it. Or would she?

"You mentioned you'd found the murder weapon?"

Araminta waited expectantly for the detective to elaborate, but just then, Jacob walked into the room with a scowl on his face.

"Really, Ivan, I hardly see that you have enough evidence to take someone into custody already!" Jacob looked back out into the hallway, where Araminta could hear a commotion.

They were arresting someone? Araminta stood and peered out, gasping when she saw two uniformed policemen leading Daphne Burgess toward the front door.

"Daphne?" Araminta spun to the detective. "Clearly you have lost your mind, young man. Why in the world would you suspect Daphne, Ivan? You've known her since you were a child!"

Ivan cleared his throat. "As I was saying, we found the murder weapon. It was a leash, Araminta. We found it in Daphne's station."

"What? I don't understand. Someone must have put it there, then." Araminta looked to Jacob for verification.

"She insists it isn't hers, but they're taking her in on

suspicion of murder anyway. I say it's a bit premature. The investigation is barely underway." Jacob gave Ivan a pointed look.

Ivan shuffled his feet slightly in the face of her censure but straightened his shoulders and met his grandfather's gaze without flinching. "This is my job, and I'm going by the book. One of the contestants witnessed that Daphne was not at her station during the time the murder occurred. Her defense? She claims to have been in the bathroom. But no one saw her in there. You and I both know she could also have been in the library, and since, so far, there is no one who knows precisely where she was…"

Poor Daphne. Obviously, she was telling the truth. Unable to let the matter lie, Araminta said, "She has no motive for murder!"

Ivan held his ground. "Ms. Bellaforte's cat was a favorite. Perhaps she wanted to cut her out of the competition?"

Araminta opened her mouth to say more, but Jacob interrupted. "Come away now, Araminta. We will see Daphne off and let her know not to worry. Ivan may have his mind set about this one, but you and I know what to do."

Following Jacob's sage advice for once, Araminta walked with him to where Daphne waited, her head held high, between two cops, who were also waiting for the detective. "Don't you worry about a thing, Daphne. I know you could never have done this—especially to better your odds in a competition!"

Daphne nodded. "Could you take care of Shaggy for me? He will be so alone and confused without me. I—"

Araminta waved the cops away and stepped in to embrace her friend. "Of course I will. Zsa Zsa, too, as now that I think about it, with Nina gone, she will need looking after as well."

Ivan stepped into the entry. "We have contacted Nina's cousin. She will be coming for Zsa Zsa this afternoon."

He nodded to the policemen who were waiting with Daphne, and they led her out the door. Ivan followed but then paused to look back at Araminta and his grandfather. "I am sorry. I know she is a friend, but until we have a reason to suspect someone else, I must do my job."

Araminta said nothing. Nor did Jacob. But the minute the door closed behind the boy, Jacob grabbed Araminta by the elbow and led her through the front parlor to Daisy's office. He pulled out his iPhone. "The boy doesn't know, but I took a few pictures of the so-called murder weapon. Have a look."

Araminta took the phone from him and enlarged the photo so she could see it better. The light-blue leash looked rather ordinary. Made of good-quality material, it was slightly better than nice. But...

"There seems to be a dark smudge, just there. Do you see it?"

Handing the phone back to Jacob, she waited while he perused the photo. He attempted to enlarge it with arthritic fingers but only succeeded in having it snap back to its smaller size. He sighed. "I will move it to my laptop later to inspect it further, but it does look like something. Do you think it's blood?"

"Maybe… except for one strange thing."

"What is that?"

"I got a good look at the body. It was evident she was strangled, but there was no blood on the wound."

"If that smudge is blood, then that only leaves two other options. The smudge was there before, or the blood is from the killer."

$\mathcal{A}$raminta was still in Daisy's office a few minutes later when Trinity came in.

"Harold is seeing to Zsa Zsa and Shaggy." Trinity looked like she'd recovered from her earlier shock of finding a body.

"That's good. But my dear girl, how are you?" Araminta rose and went to place a hand on Trinity's shoulder.

"Oh, I'm okay. Much better. She folded her hands in front of her and lowered her head. "I'm sorry about this morning."

Araminta patted her shoulder. "Well, my dear, you have nothing to be sorry about."

"I suppose, but maybe I could have handled the discovery a bit better instead of shrieking my head off and alerting the entire manor." Trinity raised her gaze to Araminta. "If I'd kept my head, I might have been able to summon you first and let you get a look at the scene, you know, before the police arrived."

"Oh! I see. Well, that is very good thinking, but I'm sure you did the right thing." Araminta would have very much liked to have had more time at the crime scene, but she could hardly expect Trinity not to react. "After all, if you'd left the body to find me, someone else might have discovered it, and the scare of a body might have been too much."

Realization dawned in Trinity's eyes. "You mean Harold?"

"Yes." Araminta rushed on to reassure Trinity that she hadn't done anything wrong. "He's a dear soul, but he does have a bit of age on him. I shudder to think what may have happened had Harold been the one to find Ms. Bellaforte."

There was a bit of skepticism in Trinity's gaze. Araminta could almost hear the girl thinking that Harold was a bit younger than Araminta, and yes, he'd needed glasses and hearing aids, but he was neither completely blind nor deaf. In fact, he was rather spry for a fellow his age, but when Trinity opened her mouth to say what her eyes had already said, Araminta would have none of it.

"No, my dear girl, you're an absolute hero," she went on, extolling several of the girl's other virtues and noting her gratitude for each, but Trinity said nothing. She merely waited.

"I am sorry about your friend, Araminta. Ms. Daphne seems like the upright type. It is easy to understand how she befriended both yourself and Mr. Jacob. She is quite likeable, and Mary, Yancy, Harold, and myself were all sad to see her taken away. You are going to help her, aren't you?"

Finally, Araminta understood. Trinity wanted to let Araminta know she knew the pain she must be feeling and would be happy to lend a hand, should Araminta need it, in whatever was required to prove Daphne's innocence and bring her back.

"Good heavens, yes!" Araminta exclaimed. "And Jacob, too, though I'm sure we won't see much of him for the next few days. He'll be too busy trying to outmaneuver me."

Trinity laughed. There was a bit of an impish twinkle in the girl's eye when she asked, "Has he ever managed to outdo you, Ms. Moorecliff?"

"Humph," Araminta grumped. "*He* would say yes, of course, but I would have to say he'd done so only when I allowed it in order to save his manly pride."

"He must be quite special to have earned the privilege of such allowance," Trinity said, but Araminta could clearly hear the hint of question in her tone.

"Jacob is a dear friend, of course, but when it comes to solving mysteries such as this one"—Araminta nudged the girl with her elbow as if notifying her she was sharing a secret— "sometimes the stubborn old coot needs a helping hand. Not that he will ever admit it."

"Of course not," Trinity agreed. "But it still must be

nice to have someone with whom to share your ideas. Someone you trust."

"Hmm," Araminta muttered. "Yes, and it would also be nice if that someone weren't always trying to get ahead of himself to gain the upper hand."

"Yes, well." Trinity fluffed the feather duster she'd held in her hand and headed toward the bookshelf. "If you need any of us to help with things, we are here for you. All of us."

Araminta felt a moment's pride for the family who surrounded her, even the extended ones because she truly did think of the staff as family. And Jacob... oh dear.

How long had she been sitting here, lost in thought, before Trinity arrived? Where had he wandered off to? She'd best hurry along and find him, Araminta decided. She didn't want him to get too far ahead of her in the investigation.

# CHAPTER SEVEN

*A*raminta left Daisy's office, her entire intent to locate Jacob. If the past was any indication, she decided as she headed toward the ballroom, he'd be sniffing about, possibly bothering the cat show competitors' owners with questions none of them would want to answer. The police had given the go-ahead to resume the competition, and everyone would be stressed out, trying to make up for lost time. Not to mention the cloud of a murder hanging over the festivities.

She was waylaid by Arun and Sasha, who came darting out from a side hallway.

"Mew!" Arun weaved in between her ankles.

"Meow!" Sasha rubbed her face on Araminta's shin.

She bent down to pet them. "Now, now, I know this is all very disturbing, but we must carry on."

"Merooo!" Arun took off down the hallway, skidding to a stop halfway down. Apparently, that was his idea of carrying on.

"Merow!" Sasha trotted down the hall, stopping in front of the bathroom and looking back at Araminta expectantly.

"Your litter boxes are in the mudroom next to the solarium." Araminta kept their litter boxes in the room that was hardly ever used. They had another area with litter boxes for the cats in the competition to use outdoors in one of the covered gazebos. Araminta had considered putting them in the cloakroom next to the ballroom but then realized that could get a little smelly.

Arun raced back to her, nipped at the tip of her shoe and then ran back down the hall.

Did he want his litter box in the bathroom, or was it something else? Daphne had said she was in the bathroom when the murder occurred. Maybe the cats had found a clue in there that would prove that.

She walked down the hall and glanced in at the floor first. No dead bodies, thankfully. She looked around, but the only thing she saw was a variety of cat hairs on the floor. She must remember to ask Trinity to vacuum. She didn't see anything out of the ordinary that might prove Daphne was in there. Even if something of hers had been here, that would only prove she'd been there but not the exact time.

"There's nothing in here. Now, you two go about your business. I need to get back to the ballroom and make sure things are running smoothly." *And that Jacob hasn't gotten too much of a head start.* She hurried off to the ballroom, leaving the cats meowing in the hallway.

Jacob was not in the ballroom when Araminta got

there. She was scanning the room for him when Millicent approached, one hand waving the air in front of her face while the other shifted and plucked the fabric of her shell-pink dress away from her chest.

"My word, it is hot today, is it not?" she declared, still fanning herself feverishly.

Araminta arched a brow—the air conditioning throughout the manor kept the temperature inside at a moderate cool. For a moment, she wondered if Millicent was feeling the heat of being guilty of murder in a manor only recently filled with police.

After all, Millicent did have every reason to be angry with Nina. The woman had practically ruined her prized feline's beautiful white fur with a nasty wad of bright-pink gum. Had she killed Nina for reducing Jasmine's chances of winning the competition? That would be a bit drastic, but one never knew.

But the leash was found in Daphne's station, and that was way on the other side of the ballroom from Millicent's station. Surely, someone would notice her going over there and rummaging about? *And what about the rose petals?* she asked herself, remembering. Those would seem to indicate something romantic.

Millicent laughed. She put a hand on Araminta's arm and explained. "Oh, don't worry that I am complaining against your hospitality, Araminta. Moorecliff Manor is perfect. It's these dratted hot flashes!"

Oh dear. Araminta quite vividly remembered how horrid those were. No matter the temperature, when you were dealing with that particular affliction, you always seemed to be on fire. She hadn't realized that Millicent was of an age to suffer from them. She was certainly very youthful, with a slim figure and full head of luxurious dark hair... except now that Araminta looked closer, she could see a touch of gray roots peeking out at the top.

Offering a commiserative smile, Araminta nodded. "I couldn't decide whether you were dealing with nature's special form of torment for females or if you were feeling the heat of being under scrutiny as a potential murderer."

Again, Millicent laughed. "You think I would stoop to murder over a blob of gum? That's not much of a motive, really, considering Jasmine is likely to win anyway, despite yesterday's sticky debacle."

Millicent's husband, Donald, had been fiddling in the bag behind Millicent's station. He finally found what he was searching for—a delicately made paper-and-lace fan. He brought it to Millicent. She took it without acknowledgment. Her expression remained distracted when he pressed the requisite "older married couple" kiss to her cheek. Still without acknowledging him, she flicked the fan open and started to fan herself with it. When she turned back to Araminta, her easy, open smile said she wasn't worried.

"Besides, you know me better than that, Minta," she said. "You and I both know there are things far worse than death, yeah?"

Donald walked away, back to Millicent's station. Millicent followed Donald with her eyes for a moment, then she flicked the fan closed, turned back to Araminta, and winked. "My motto is to let them live. A long, long life fraught with multiple deliveries of well-deserved karma, or fate, is a far sweeter form of revenge."

Araminta chuckled. "At our age, allowing karma to follow its natural course is without doubt the best of all outcomes, I agree."

Millicent cut her eyes back to her husband. She nodded and started to fan herself again. "I did see something interesting, though," she admitted.

Araminta was suddenly all ears, though she pretended an interest in the other contestants, who were all busy at their stations. "Oh? Do tell."

"It happened yesterday, actually. I saw Nina... she was flirting with Clint—leaning across his table, laughing, trying to lure him into conversation." Millicent shook her head. "Guess he wasn't interested, though. He ignored her as best he could, but when that didn't work, the poor man practically pushed her away. She wasn't too happy about it."

Araminta gave her a look. "What do you mean?"

"She was furious. Like red-in-the-face furious." She smiled, but this time it was a cattish type of smile. Millicent shrugged. "I don't think she handles rejection very well. Maybe she tried again, and he... well, probably not, but you know what I'm saying."

Yes, Araminta did. Millicent was saying there was a possibility that Clint had killed Nina in the library because she would not leave him alone. Could her romantic interest in him explain the rose petals in the library? Maybe. Araminta sighed.

"There always seem to be more questions than answers when it comes to something like this," she told Millicent. What she didn't say, however, was that she had a feeling, despite Millicent's casual drop of information about Clint and Nina's obvious disagreement yesterday, that she was still hiding something.

"Exactly," Millicent said. "But you could always talk to him. One never knows what one might discover through a simple conversation."

"Oh, I absolutely will speak with him soon," Araminta promised, though once again, she had a feeling what Millicent wasn't saying was speaking volumes. Though she wanted to give her the benefit of the doubt, Araminta couldn't shake the feeling something was missing in their conversation.

# CHAPTER EIGHT

Jacob still hadn't put in an appearance in the ballroom since Nina's body had been removed from the library. Millicent had wandered back to her station and was busy crooning to Jasmine while her husband, Donald, hovered close by. Araminta saw him give Millicent a brush for the cat's fur and wondered if abundant brushing would fix the mess made in Jasmine's otherwise perfect coat by the gum, but she was soon distracted by loud meowling from Zsa Zsa's cage.

Araminta made a circuit of the ballroom, paying special attention to the various leashes the cat owners had at their stations. Everyone had more than one, and most were of simple construction very similar to the leash that was used to strangle Nina. It was impossible to tell if anyone was missing a leash.

Harold had taken Shaggy upstairs first and apparently had yet to return for Zsa Zsa. Perhaps that was for the best, as he'd just have to lug the cat back down when Nina's cousin arrived to collect her.

Nina's station was near Clint Sterling, and Araminta decided that a conversation with him was in order. Millicent had roused her curiosity. Perhaps Clint could settle it.

"You there. Mr. Sterling? Hello," Araminta called as she waved to him and headed over. "Are you enjoying the competition thus far?"

He gave her a look Araminta felt was loaded with unspoken sarcasm then said, "With the exception of this morning's disturbing event, yes, I am enjoying the opportunity to be here. Your home is extraordinary, and the service of your staff is without fault."

Araminta noted the edge of fine steel lacing his tone. Despite his words to the contrary, he clearly found fault with something. "The murder of Ms. Bellaforte was quite a shock to all of us. Did you know her well?"

Clint tugged at the long sleeves of his formal white linen shirt, which was tucked into the top of his midnight-black trousers. He then bent to rummage through a bag beneath his station, momentarily avoiding her question, although she wasn't sure whether or not he had done so purposefully. Araminta thought he must be about to do as Millicent had and brush out his cat, but a few seconds later, he straightened and snapped on a pair of purple latex gloves.

"I did not," he finally answered in regard to his personal acquaintance with Nina then added, "Though

Ms. Bellaforte clearly had hoped to remedy our unfamiliarity."

His tone was still cutting. Araminta thought she detected a bit of a sneer in it as well. Her brow rose. "I take it you were not amenable to her more... shall we say *familiar* company?"

"Not at all." He retrieved the cat comb Araminta had thought he would bring out before. Clint checked his gloves once more, and when he noticed she was watching him do so, he hurried to explain. "I wear the gloves, unlike the rest of your contestants, because it ensures there are no contaminants such as oils and whatnot coming from my hands that will leave a residue on Loughley's fur."

Araminta nodded to let him know she understood his reasons, but he did not notice because he'd already begun to comb the cat, so she said, "Of course. You are very attentive to details and excruciatingly thorough, Mr. Sterling. Your father must be very proud."

"Shedding again." He frowned down at the fluff of solid brown hair then sighed. "Ms. Moorecliff, my father's pride is neither here nor there. What matters at the moment is whether or not your judges recognize fine breeding."

"Precisely," Araminta agreed, but she couldn't help but notice the fur that had fallen onto the table as he combed. It seemed Mr. Sterling was as interested in conversing about his father as much as he was about Nina Bellaforte—which was not at all.

"I do have one other question regarding Ms.

Bellaforte, however. Or, more precisely, Zsa Zsa," Araminta said before he could object or send her away. "Do you know if Nina fed her or took her to the litter box area this morning before…?"

Clint shook his head. "I haven't a clue what Ms. Bellaforte may or may not have done with either her time or her contestant before her untimely demise. How could I? I have been focused on my cat practically the entire morning, other than those few brief moments when I stepped away to get water for Loughley."

It was at that moment Araminta realized Clint was probably telling the truth. He was so caught up with and distressed over his own contestant, she wondered why he wasn't shedding himself. Perhaps he was, she thought, her gaze flitting quickly to his full head of salt-and-pepper hair.

*Now is not the time for inspecting the condition of your guest's hair,* Araminta silently scolded herself. *There has been a murder in the manor. Concentrate on that. And on finding Jacob.*

After thanking Clint for his time, she decided to try to get some information on one of the clues. The rose petals. There had only been a few, maybe enough for one rose. Had the killer plucked a rose out of the many vases around the manor to present it to Nina?

She made a circuit of the lower level of the manor, paying attention to the floral arrangements placed about, but not one vase sported the type of roses that would account for the petals found at this morning's crime scene.

Had Jacob found anything? she wondered. But

then, if he had, she knew he likely would not tell her. Instead, he would wait until an opportunity presented itself wherein he could point out what she had missed by employing her own method: interrogation in lieu of investigation. Unlike himself, of course, who preferred to seek and follow the physical clues. As if the proper steps to solving a crime must always go his way.

Pshawing the thought, Araminta climbed the stairs to her suite on the second floor. Poor Shaggy would be beside himself, and Zsa Zsa would be delivered to her room soon. She should comfort them. Besides, the view was beautiful from her balcony, and the upper floor would be much quieter than here, where the comings and goings from the ballroom continued to distract her from her mission.

Nina was dead, and someone from the competition was a killer, but who? The answer continued to elude her, which meant right now, she really needed to be alone in her room, where she could think.

# CHAPTER NINE

 run sat in front of the marble fireplace in Araminta's room and groomed himself as he listened to Shaggy wail about how distressed he was. You'd think the cat would just enjoy the moment, as he was sprawled out in a puddle of warm sun atop Araminta's delightfully soft silk bedspread, his fluffy tail swishing back and forth as he meowed incessantly.

"I'm just so distraught! Daphne is my best friend, and I don't know what I will do without her."

"Don't worry," Sasha consoled him. "Araminta is on the case. She will find the real killer and get Daphne out of jail."

Arun hopped up on the windowsill and looked outside. It was a sunny day, and Yancy, the gardener, was pruning the azaleas. It would be a fine day to lounge under the oak tree and bat around some acorns. But first, they had work to do. "If only Araminta would listen to us. I think she's a bit distracted with the cat show."

"You mean about the bathroom?" Sasha asked. "She did look in."

"Yes, but she didn't see what we wanted her to see."

"Maybe Codger has had better luck with Jacob."

Just then, the door opened, and Harold came in carrying a large cat carrier with Zsa Zsa inside.

"Here now, are you cats enjoying yourselves?" He looked at Arun then Sasha then Shaggy as he set the cat carrier on the floor with a grunt.

"Meow," Arun said.

"Mew," Sasha added

"No." Shaggy's meow sounded almost human, and Harold frowned at him before opening the door to the crate.

Zsa Zsa burst out and ran under the bed, turning around and peering out from under the bed skirt with her luminous eyes.

"You cats be nice to her," Harold said. "She's had a big loss."

He turned and left, closing the door behind him.

"We're so sorry about your human." Sasha's blue eyes were full of sympathy.

"Thank you. It's been very trying." Zsa Zsa inched her way out from under the bed.

"Her human? What about *mine*?" Shaggy said from atop the bed.

Zsa Zsa's eyes widened when she saw Shaggy, and she hissed. "Your human killed my human."

Shaggy sprang up on all fours. "She did not!"

Zsa Zsa humped her back and hissed again. "Did too!"

"Now hold on!" Arun didn't want a cat fight in Araminta's bedroom. He shuddered at the image of shattered vases, clawed drapes, and ruined bedding. Somehow, he would be to blame, so he needed to calm the cats down. "Did either of you witness this murder?"

"No," they both admitted.

"It may not have been Daphne. Let's not go off half clawed." Arun turned to Zsa Zsa. "Now, what did you see?"

Sasha looked dejected. "Nothing. My human is very umm…. social. But this morning, she seemed a bit more serious. Said she had to get a look at something to prove a theory. Whatever that means."

Sasha and Arun exchanged a glance. Araminta thought it was a lovers' quarrel, but maybe she was on the wrong track.

"What about you, Shaggy? What did you see?" Arun asked.

Shaggy sighed and flopped back down. "Nada. My human took me to the litter boxes and then said she needed to use the litter box herself. So naturally, I used the downtime to catch some Z's."

"So she wasn't at the grooming station before you heard the scream?" Sasha asked.

"Nope. But I know she couldn't have done it."

"Araminta thinks she is innocent as well," Arun said.

"Well, the police don't," Zsa Zsa pointed out.

"Yes, but Araminta is usually right about these things," Sasha said. "Now, think hard. Did any of you see or hear anything that might point us to the identity of the killer?"

"I don't know if this will help identify the killer, but there was something." Shaggy sat up, suddenly interested in imparting any knowledge that might help clear Daphne. "Shortly after Daphne left, my slumber was interrupted by someone rummaging in the bags under the grooming station. I assumed it was my human coming back to give me a treat, so I shook myself awake. Except it wasn't Daphne. No one was there. And I didn't get any treat."

"That must have been the killer planting the leash!" Sasha said.

Shaggy gasped.

Arun jumped up on the bed next to him. "Did you see who it was? Maybe catch a scent or a flutter of clothing? Anything?"

Shaggy deflated. "Sadly, no."

"Well, at least that proves it wasn't Daphne," Sasha said. "She would hardly plant the murder weapon in her own bags."

"True," Zsa Zsa agreed. "But if it wasn't Daphne, then who was it?"

# CHAPTER TEN

It was afternoon before Araminta finally caught up with Jacob. She'd spent quite a bit of time in her room, consoling Zsa Zsa and Shaggy. Sasha and Arun had appeared quite jealous, trying to lead her out of the room the whole time. Of course, she lavished them with attention as well, but the four cats seemed dreadfully out of sorts anyway.

Jacob was in the large hallway outside the library, squinting into the dimness of the room as if he saw something but could not quite make out what it was.

"Searching for more clues, are we?" Araminta asked.

"What? Yes, actually, I was, but there are no more to be found. At least not here," he said, turning to peer at her now through squinted lids. "And what of you? Have you spent the morning interrogating every possible suspect?"

Araminta knew Jacob much preferred following the

clues to questioning the people when a crime occurred, but that didn't stop her from rolling her eyes at his accusatory tone. He claimed the *clues* never lied but *people* often did.

Araminta preferred the opposite, and for very good reasons. There were so many facets to people—facets Jacob always seemed wont to overlook. Expressions, body language, and a hundred little tells that might (and often did) put her gut instinct on a hunch that, more times than not, led her to the solving of the crime.

"I've spoken with a few of the show's attendees," she hedged. "I've also taken a lengthy stroll around the manor, searching this morning's floral arrangements for roses that might account for the petals found beside Nina's body, but there are none."

Jacob bobbed his head up and down then rubbed his hands together. There was also a glint of mischievous glee in his eyes that was hard for her well-trained gaze to miss.

"Well, there's a start in the right direction, anyway. The clues will never lead us astray, m'dear."

Araminta's eyes narrowed. "Are you beating around the bush in an attempt to offhandedly tell me you've found a clue, Jacob?"

His shoulder lifted in a nonchalant shrug. "Perhaps. Or perhaps it is nothing."

Araminta waited all of five seconds before demanding, "Well? You know you can't string me along, Jacob Hershey. If you've found something, you'd best be out with it."

He laughed at that. "Tsk-tsk. Still demanding, I see."

Araminta wanted to roll her eyes, to shake her head. Instead, she said, "Just trying to be thorough, Jacob, and as I've witnessed from you, one can't figure out a crime if there are clues that another refuses to reveal."

Playing him like a fiddle, that's what she was doing. Araminta had figured out long ago that if she subtly pointed out how she was trying to follow his tutelage by combing through every possible link in addition to her own interrogation, he would crumble like a cookie.

His brow rose.

Fighting back a smile, she waited. It didn't take long for him to cave, proving yet again she was right.

"I noted there is a bit of brown residue in your bathroom sink, Minty," he said. "I'm not sure when it got there, but perhaps you should have someone clean it."

Brown residue? The first thing she thought of was Donald. And hair dye. And the bad color job he was currently sporting. Had he touched it up in the bathroom sink? Gross. The second thing she thought of was how Arun and Sasha had been making such a ruckus there earlier. She'd peered in, but had she looked at the sink? No, she'd been too busy looking for something of Daphne's and worrying that there was a body on the floor.

If the cats had wanted her to see the brown residue, it might be important.

She started toward the bathroom in question, asking over her shoulder as she went, "You did swab it, yes?"

Jacob, who followed just as she had assumed he would, affirmed her guess with a pat to his jacket pocket. "While wearing gloves, even."

His eyes narrowed, but when she turned to praise him for being thorough, she could see a glimmer of humor in them. "I did not fall off the turnip truck just yesterday, either, you know."

"Of course not," Araminta said, as if it was ridiculous for him to even think she would think such a thing. Then she grinned. "That's why I asked, Jacob. You're getting so decrepit these days, old man, I thought you may have forgotten what constitutes proper investigative protocol."

He drew up, pretending offense. "Me decrepit? And whose knees are so creaky these days even the delightfully scented bath oil you use could not free them up?"

Araminta felt a blush creep over her cheeks to hear that he found her bath oil delightful, but like him, she pretended she didn't care. "My knees are fine. The same as your logic."

"Of course they are," Jacob said, giving in.

Araminta inspected the stain. It didn't look like blood; maybe it was some kind of makeup. Hopefully, Jacob could get his swab analyzed. She opened the cabinet under the vanity and took out a cloth and cleanser. She certainly wasn't going to summon Trinity for this little job. Just a few scrubs, and it was gone.

"Looks like you are a woman of many talents,"

Jacob commented as she put the cleaning products away and turned to leave the bathroom.

Araminta was ready with a sarcastic comment, but the fond look in Jacob's gaze distracted her, and she almost ran into Harold, who was standing just outside the bathroom. Ignoring his confusion at finding the two of them together in what should be a single-occupancy room, Araminta asked, "Yes? Did you need something, Harold?"

Not daring to comment on the odd situation, he merely nodded. "You've a visitor. Miss Nina's cousin, Muriel. She's in the front parlor. She's come to collect Zsa Zsa. I'll get the cat from your room."

# CHAPTER ELEVEN

uriel Chase, Nina's cousin on her mother's side, was a short, stout woman who moved as if the very world were in her path and she had full intent to clear it. Bulldozer was mild as a personal description, Araminta thought. Rather, a combination bulldozer and steamroller. While she contemplated whether or not there existed such a machine, Jacob pushed around her to introduce himself. Araminta snapped out of her momentary reverie out of sheer necessity. It would not do to allow Jacob the upper hand here.

"Mrs. Chase," she said, holding out her hand to the woman. "It is a pleasure to meet you, though one wishes not to have done so under such circumstances."

There was no reason not to bring up Nina's murder right away. Muriel was here, after all, because there was no one else to collect her poor deceased cousin's cat. Muriel agreed.

"Quite so, though I have to admit I'm surprised the girl hasn't come to a bad end before now, the way she jumped from bedroom to bedroom, husband to husband." She looked around the parlor then back at Araminta. "Where is Zsa Zsa? The poor darling must be in shock."

Araminta's brow furrowed. "Nina was married? I wasn't aware…"

Muriel cut her a look. Her lips twisted. "I did not say the husbands were hers."

Jacob's cough was not missed. "Perhaps I should have Mary prepare tea?"

Araminta nodded. "Thank you, Jacob. Please do."

He hurried out of the room, but Araminta wasn't surprised. The old scoundrel. He didn't care one whit for the nattering of females and was quite happy to run about like a hired hand if it would get him out of the conversation. As soon as she was sure he'd moved out of earshot, Araminta patted Muriel's hand like a coconspirator and motioned toward a chair near the window. "Won't you sit? I'd love to ask a few questions about your niece while we wait for tea, and Zsa Zsa of course. That is if you don't mind?"

Muriel didn't. Mind, that is. She started talking the instant her bottom settled in the chair and barely hesitated to sip at her tea when Trinity brought a tray around. "Her latest affair was the worst, if I do say so myself." She tsked. "That Copperfield fellow was leading her on but good. He wanted what Nina was all too willing to offer, but no matter how she begged and pleaded, he refused point-blank to leave his wife."

*Copperfield?* Araminta blinked. "You don't mean Donald Copperfield?"

"You know him?" Muriel asked, her eyes gone suddenly narrow. She gave Araminta a quick once-over then sniffed. If she'd been a glasses wearer, Araminta was sure she would have used that precise moment to shove her lenses higher on the bridge of her nose. As it were, she merely lifted her chin, her expression now one of barely suppressed disdain. "I wouldn't have thought it of you, Ms. Moorecliff, but if you say you know him, too, then perhaps poor Nina had more competition than she'd thought."

Araminta barely had time to register the fact that Nina's cousin had just told her Donald and Nina were having an affair. She'd only just connected the younger woman–older man scenario in her mind with the hair dye in the bathroom sink. Was Donald the reason for the dye in the sink? Was he trying to look younger to impress Nina and therefore maintain their affair?

Harold's gasp of shock reminded Araminta that Muriel's words could be taken as a grave insult. He stood in the doorway with a tote bag of cat supplies in one hand and the cat carrier, with Zsa Zsa slumbering inside, in the other.

Araminta stuck a finger into the carrier to pet the cat's silky bluish-gray fur. Zsa Zsa slitted one eye open and snorted before curling into a tighter ball. Araminta turned to Muriel. "Here's Zsa Zsa, Mrs. Chase. Would you prefer we leave her here with you, or would you like Harold to see her settled in your car?"

Muriel's pert nose wrinkled. "The sedan, if you please. I'll have to deal with her plenty once we're home. No sense starting until one must, I say."

Araminta felt sorry for the cat and almost pulled the carrier away, offering to care for the cat herself. She worried Muriel might not provide it with a loving home, considering she hadn't even bothered to pet the poor thing. But she didn't want to stifle the conversation. Maybe later, she could make sure the cat was being properly cared for.

"Harold, could you take Zsa Zsa out to Mrs. Chase's car, please, and see that she has food and water for the journey?"

Harold moved to do just that, and Araminta turned back to Muriel.

"You seem not to mind a bit of frank conversation, Mrs. Chase. Tell me about Nina's relationship with Mr. Copperfield. You mention she wanted him to, ah, to leave his wife. Do you think he may have become angry at her for her continued attempts? Angry enough to kill her?"

"I don't think there's anything to question, really." Muriel took a second sip of her tea then set the delicate bone china cup and saucer aside. "To my recollection, not a day has gone by when Nina didn't request Donald's full attention, and conversely, no day passed without his adamant refusal."

For the first time since Araminta had entered the

room, a brief shadow of what might have been sadness passed over the woman's face. "Maybe she finally pushed him too hard and he decided it was time to be rid of her once and for all? Of course, he wouldn't dare risk his wife finding out about the two of them, so murder truly makes the most sense."

Araminta wasn't sure if she agreed with the woman, but then, she had only just learned about Donald's affair with Nina herself. But what if *Millicent* had already discovered her husband's infidelity? There was a motive for murder if she'd ever seen one. She knew Nina and Donald were sneaking around together, so she waited until the morning routine for the cat show was in full swing and slipped out to kill her herself.

It made sense, Araminta decided, and yet it did not. Millicent had not seemed overly fond of Donald. In fact, it appeared she might not mind being rid of him. Had that been an act? She was pretty sure Millicent wouldn't have wanted Donald to leave her for Nina— no, she surely would not have wished for such a thing because if Donald should go, so, too, would his money.

## CHAPTER TWELVE

With Muriel gone, Araminta had a few minutes to think over everything she'd said. Donald and Nina were engaged in an extramarital fling. Nina wanted Donald to leave Millicent. He refused, but she wouldn't take no for an answer. He was a likely suspect, but somehow, that didn't seem like enough motive to kill her. Would Donald be that terrified of Nina exposing the affair to Millicent?

Maybe Millicent *was* a better suspect. Would she have killed Nina because she was trying to steal her husband? And if it truly *was* Millicent who had done the dastardly deed despite her insistence to the contrary, why frame Daphne?

"Aunt Minta?"

The quietly voiced question brought Araminta back to the present. Stephanie stood in the doorway. Her shoulder-length blond hair was highlighted from summer days in the sun, and she was wearing a T-shirt and jeans with smudges of dirt. No doubt she'd been helping Yancy in the garden again.

"Stephanie! I'm sorry. I was woolgathering, I'm afraid."

Stephanie nodded and smiled. "We have gathered enough wool that I think we shall all soon have an entirely new wardrobe."

Araminta chuckled. "I believe you are right, my dear. This murder is quite the conundrum."

"Everything will sort itself soon enough. You've only just begun to piece things together, but I'm certain it is just a matter of time." She nodded as if to convince Araminta of her certainty. "You always find a way to put things to rights."

"Thank you, sweetheart," Araminta said. She pushed up out of the chair. "Was there a problem in the ballroom? I'm afraid I simply dropped straight into thought once Mrs. Chase departed."

She noticed a bit of a twinkle in Stephanie's eyes. "No problem. Only a new arrival. A guest. Harold said I should come and fetch you."

"A guest? But I thought everyone who had RSVP'd had arrived already. Who could it be?"

Stephanie chuckled. "I shouldn't say. In fact, Harold will probably be upset with me for doing so, but I think I shall simply deal with his scowls. Your good friend Bertie is here. When I left the ballroom, he was chatting with Jacob."

Araminta's happy gasp was audible. "Oh, Steph,

you know I am the only one who is allowed to call him that."

Stephanie grinned. Wrapping her arm through Araminta's, she tugged her aunt toward the door. "Very well. I promise to call him Bart, or Bartholomew, or Mr. Belamie if you prefer, but I think we should go and rescue him from Jacob and Harold. You know how those two can be."

Bartholomew Belamie was ninety if he was a day old, but as she approached the two gentlemen with Stephanie at her side, Araminta had to admit he still had the same vivacity he'd had when they were younger. His eyes sparkled at some wit he'd shared with Jacob, but his eyes lit even more once he realized she was there.

"Araminta! What a pleasure to see you." He reached around Jacob for her hand, which he promptly brought up to his lips for a kiss. "You get more beautiful with each year that passes."

Araminta felt a warm blush heat her cheeks, which was more due to her niece witnessing her appreciation of the man before her than to his words. "Oh, please, Bertie. You know there's no need for such praise with me. We've known each other far too long for that."

Jacob's clearing of his throat broke in. "We were talking about Daphne, Araminta. You remember, right? Our dear friend who has been unfairly thrown into jail?"

Araminta brushed aside his bluster. "Of course, Jacob. As if I would have forgotten. Daphne is never far from my thoughts, I can assure you. As a matter of fact…"

Jacob took her arm and tugged her forward. "If you'll excuse us, Bart, there's a recent visit we need to discuss."

"No trouble at all. My assistant, Stella, is just getting our things in our rooms, and I should see if she needs help," Bart said.

Rather than fuss over Jacob's obvious attempt to pull her away from their old friend, Araminta nodded to Stephanie. "Steph, darling, won't you give Mr. Belamie and his assistant a tour of the grounds once they are settled? There is something rather important I'd like to discuss with Jacob."

As they walked away, Araminta followed Jacob to an alcove near the doors to the ballroom.

"You still blush every time you see him. Gives you away every time."

Araminta ignored his comment, preferring instead to talk about Daphne. "Muriel says Donald and Nina were having an affair. The rose petals make perfect sense if she was intent upon staging a seduction…"

"Do you have feelings for him, Minta? After all these years?" Jacob asked.

Araminta blinked. "Who? Bertie?"

He nodded. "Of course I do. He is a good friend, Jacob, and his wit and whimsy always make me smile."

Jacob snorted. "I'm surprised the two of you never absconded to some island paradise. Him with his jewels and you with his wit and whimsy."

Araminta pinned him with a look. Bert was a fine jeweler and a good friend, but Araminta had never been attracted to him that way. "Paradise never appealed to me so much as the thrill of a good mystery. I've always preferred finding answers to having someone else hand them to me—regardless of the quality sterling platter they'd be served upon."

Jacob grunted as if he didn't believe her. "Muriel... she seemed convinced of an affair between one of your guests and the deceased. Did she say anything else?"

"Nothing that would be of particular interest to you. I was thinking. If they were having an affair, the rose petals make sense, especially if Nina were intent upon seduction." Araminta drifted into thought again. "Poor girl. She set the scene for her own murder."

"If Donald *is* the murderer," Jacob pointed out. "There are yet clues to be uncovered, I'm sure of it. Why frame Daphne? That is the question we still need answers to."

"We?" Araminta gave him a look. "Do you mean to say you still don't have everything figured out?"

"I'd be lying to say otherwise, but I'd remind you to note that neither do you. If you had, you wouldn't be subtly trying to convince me to join you in a conversation with Donald."

Araminta chuckled while continuing to do just that. "Why, Jacob. How very astute you are!"

# CHAPTER THIRTEEN

*A*raminta wasted no time getting to the point with Donald. "Mr. Copperfield, how are you holding up? You must be devastated by Ms. Bellaforte's death. It must be difficult to restrain your grief with your wife so close at hand."

Donald's brow rose and then quickly folded into a scowl. "Nina—Ms. Bellaforte—was a regular on the cat show circuit. She will be missed."

Jacob, bless him, nodded and then said, "I suspect more so by you than the rest, if Mrs. Chase is to be believed."

Araminta wanted to kick him and hug him at the same time. Kick him for his blunt segue to the affair Donald was having with Nina before she was ready and hug him for the same because he'd saved her time. "Muriel suggested there was more to your and Nina's acquaintance than the circuit, Mr. Copperfield."

He seemed about to protest, but then he shoved his

hands into his pockets and nodded. "Yes. Nina and I were having an affair, but I didn't kill her."

"You didn't?"

He shook his head. "The facts will bear out my truth. Consider the logistics if you will. Simply going from the ballroom to the library and then to Ms. Daphne's station—it would take more time than I've accounted for in my statement to the police. You see, I was at a board meeting all morning and arrived back at the manor just as they were carting poor Daphne away. I can prove it down to the exact minute. When I arrived, I came straight here to the ballroom and Millicent's station."

Jacob caught Araminta's glance, surreptitiously letting her know he would check into Donald's whereabouts himself.

"Besides," Donald continued, as if he hadn't noticed the silent communication between the two. "Why would any decent sort of murderer walk through the entire ballroom while it is filled with people and while holding the murder weapon?"

There was sarcasm in his tone when he said, "Yes, that is precisely what I would have had to have done if I had killed Nin—Ms. Bellaforte. You see, Millicent's station is there."

He pointed out the obvious, but Araminta's shrewd gaze followed the motion, calculating.

"But I would have needed to pass her *and* two other contestants' stations in order to hide the leash among Ms. Daphne's things and in plain view of everyone who cared to look. Far too risky, yes? Therefore, it makes no sense."

Araminta had to admit it did seem he was right. No murderer who hoped to escape unscathed would dare traipse through a room full of witnesses carrying the very weapon he'd used to commit such a heinous crime even if they could somehow hide it in their pocket or a bag.

"Despite what you may have heard, I am rather intelligent, Ms. Moorecliff," Donald said, his gaze darting toward his wife. "But if you're interested to know who might actually have wanted to get both Nina and Daphne out of the way, perhaps you should look no further than there."

He tilted his head in the opposite direction, and Araminta followed his gaze. "Stephen Roy?"

Jacob arched a brow and nodded. "Yes, of course. His cat would be a shoo-in for largest feline if Daphne's were out of the running, and with Zsa Zsa gone as well, that might be enough for him to win the entire show. That's motive, Araminta."

Donald crossed his arms over his chest, his expression smug. "Precisely."

"I should have thought of Stephen earlier," Araminta confessed to Jacob a few minutes later as they walked away from Donald. "I remember seeing him arguing with Viv—you remember her? Trinity said Viv took over for Tony Romano, and… I think he owes money to the crime syndicate. Maybe he has to win the competition to pay off whoever has something on him?

"It *must* be him, Jacob. Why else would a man like him have joined the competition?" Eyes wide, she turned to Jacob. "Stephen Roy must be Nina Bellaforte's killer!"

"Well then, you must either produce evidence to prove your hunch or force a confession from him," Jacob told her. His expression said he had his doubts. There was no substantial evidence that pointed to Stephen, and thus, Jacob would not seriously consider him a suspect. But neither would he stand in Araminta's way. He took both her hands in his and gave one a fond pat. "I shall leave you to it."

A confession, yes, Araminta decided. It was the only thing that would work. She knew, just as Jacob did, that there was no evidence that pointed precisely to Stephen. The murder weapon had no fingerprints or at least none that she'd heard about. And with Jacob's connections still to the police, she was sure he would have heard if that were the case. Of course, there was still the smudge on the leash. Perhaps that was unrelated to the murder, but Araminta didn't think so. If it had been the killer's blood, though, the police would have been able to narrow things down quite quickly and would have come for another suspect.

Stephen's station was so very near to Daphne's. It would have been easy for him to stash the leash there after he'd killed Nina in the library. Now, she simply had to get him to admit it.

Yes, forcing a confession from Mr. Roy was precisely

what she would do. But how? An idea struck, and she hurried out of the ballroom to find Trinity.

After she had explained her thought that Mr. Roy must be Nina's killer to Trinity, Araminta told her she planned to trap him into confessing. "I wondered if you might help me?"

"Of course," Trinity told her. "Though I'm not certain what I could possibly do to help you force him into admitting murder."

Araminta almost grinned. This was an area of interrogation wherein she shone, if she did think so herself. "You've seen the man, Trinity. He's very nervous."

"We call those types of people 'fidgety,'" Trinity told her.

"Yes, fidgety. A bit skittish. Which leads me to think he might easily be confused. If the two of us were to go to him and ask him several back-to-back questions, it should throw him off guard. I'm hoping…"

Trinity's eyes widened. "You're hoping to shake him up enough with the seemingly unrelated questions that he will accidentally confess when you ask him about Nina because he's thinking about something else."

"Brilliant girl!" Araminta said, her tone filled with pride over the girl's cleverness. "Will you help me?"

Trinity nodded. "Absolutely."

# CHAPTER FOURTEEN

It took only a moment to find Stephen once Araminta and Trinity reached the ballroom. He was lounging near his station, watching as the judges spoke with Clint Sterling about his exotic Bengal.

"Mr. Roy, this is Trinity. She's an old friend of Vivianne's. Have the two of you been introduced?"

He stood and extended his hand first to Araminta and then to Trinity. "Wonderful contest, Ms. Moorecliff. Thank you for allowing us to assemble in your beautiful home for this auspicious event. As for Miss Trinity, we have not, but I can assure you it is my utmost pleasure to make her acquaintance."

Despite the man's obvious overdoing of the moment, Trinity actually blushed. "Mr. Roy, you've a lovely feline entered in the show. Can you tell me about him?"

"Ah, Bjorn," he said. His eyes brightened. It was clear to Araminta he genuinely cared about his pet.

"Bjorn is a Norwegian Forest cat. Aside from his coloring, he looks quite like a lion with his fluffy mane, don't you think?"

The cat was outrageously fluffy and big too. His smoke-colored hair stuck out from his black face similar to a mane, and tufts of hair sprang from his ears. He had extraordinarily long whiskers and sharp green eyes that watched her every move like a lion sizing up its prey.

"Indeed, he does." Araminta took a step away from the cat.

"We haven't seen you or Bjorn at the show during previous years, Mr. Roy," Trinity prodded. "I would have thought with a cat as glorious as Bjorn, you'd have entered every year."

"I would never have considered entering Bjorn in a contest, but Viv, she thinks the best should be acknowledged." His eyes sought and found Vivianne, who was talking to a contestant in the corner. He gave her a slow once-over, smiling with appreciation all the while. The corner of one side of his mouth tilted upward. "I find I must agree."

"Vivianne is the reason you entered Bjorn into the cat show?" Araminta asked. She sent Trinity a knowing look.

Stephen shrugged. "A guy like myself, these type of events are not my usual scene, you know? But I must admit being here with Bjorn and the other contestants and their owners... Viv was right. It has helped to take the stress off."

"So you're not here entirely because you want to please Vivianne?" Araminta asked.

"Ah, not so much, Ms. Moorecliff, but if me being here makes her happy, I'm happy, you know? But it's more because, with what I do, I find a need to chill. To unwind from time to time, you know? Like relax? Have some fun…?"

"And the prize money doesn't hurt," Trinity added with a smile. The show raised a lot for charity through sponsor donations, but there was also a twenty-five-thousand-dollar prize for the winner. "Right, Mr. Roy?"

Stephen's eyes shuttered. He shrugged and looked at the floor. "The money, it's nice enough."

Sensing she'd found her moment, Araminta asked, "You need the money, Mr. Roy?"

His chin rose, and he peered at her, his gaze piercing. "You think I come here because I need money?"

Araminta nodded. "As a matter of fact, I do, now that you mention it. You see, I saw you arguing with Vivianne the day you arrived, and we know Vivianne took over for the … for Tony. You owe them money, don't you, Mr. Roy?"

Stephen straightened his shoulders, enlarged his stance, and crossed his arms over his chest. "I don't understand. Are you accusin' me of something, Ms. Moorecliff?"

Araminta barely refrained from nodding. "You owe the mob money, Mr. Roy, and that's why you killed Nina and framed Daphne. With the two of them out of the way, Bjorn has a much better chance of winning and you an easy way to collect the cash you need."

Stephen's eyes widened, and for a moment, Araminta was sure she'd found him out. Then he laughed.

"You think I owe Tony?" He laughed harder.

Araminta said nothing.

Finally, his laughter dwindled until only an amused smile remained. "My dear Ms. Moorecliff, I don't *owe* money. I *collect* money. Look, if youse know Tony the way you say you do, then you know his—ah—*organization* could never run itself, right? If you knows what I mean, and I think youse do… "

He leaned close and thumbed himself in the chest. "That's where I come in, yeah? I take care of Tony's business. Viv takes care of the books, and she takes care of me."

After a moment more of feeling Araminta out with nothing more than his gaze, Stephen said, "Feel free to verify with Viv if you need to, but—ah—I do hope this little bit of professional knowledge won't interfere with what Bjorn and me are doin' here, okay? I find I am quite enjoying the festivities, so thank you again for lettin' us be here amongst ya."

Araminta glanced at Trinity. Her eyes were wide, and her smile was frozen in place, and it was obvious why. Stephen Roy didn't owe the local crime syndicate money. He was their new boss. Not only that, Araminta had more or less just accused this very powerful man of murder.

Shaking off her surprise from Stephen's revelation,

Araminta cleared her throat. "I understand, and of course nothing you've said will disqualify Bjorn from the competition, Mr. Roy. Yet I have to ask… "

"Anything." Stephen smiled.

For a moment, Araminta was worried he might feel she owed him something if he filled her request, but in the end, she decided it would be worth the risk to clear Daphne. "Did you see anything suspicious in the ballroom this morning? Anything at all that might help us identify Ms. Bellaforte's killer?"

He shrugged. "I was here since just before the shouting started. The only thing I saw that might've been a bit shifty? Mrs. Copperfield over by the French doors. She was there for quite some time, fanning herself. Does that a lot, to my knowledge. Maybe she was the killer's lookout?"

The French doors! Araminta immediately turned to look. Arun and Sasha were there already, strutting back and forth in front of the doors with their tails high. Was it possible her beloved pets already knew whatever Stephen wasn't quite sure of? With those two doing their dance before the doors, she was sure, if nothing else, she would at least find another clue.

"It has been a pleasure speaking with you, Mr. Roy," Araminta said. Excusing herself, she hurried straight over to the doors, leaving Trinity to make her own excuses to extricate herself from the conversation.

# CHAPTER FIFTEEN

$\mathcal{S}$asha shot out into the garden as soon as Araminta pushed open the doors, almost knocking Jacob off his feet in her eagerness to get into the sunshine. Arun followed, forcing Jacob to quickly twist in the other direction to stay on his feet.

"Oh! Bless you, Jacob. I'm sorry. The poor darlings are in such a rush," she said, holding out her hands to help steady him. Once he had his balance and Sasha and Arun had disappeared into the garden, Araminta peered at him curiously. "What are you doing out here?"

Jacob turned and pointed to another set of similar doors farther down the garden wall that led back into the manor from a curved stone patio. "Codger led me out here. Apparently, there is more than one way to get from the library to the ballroom."

Araminta stared at the door, where Sasha, Arun, and Codger were now sitting with looks of satisfaction on their faces. So that was why the cats had been pacing around the French doors. They were trying to tell her something!

"You think the killer may have gone through the garden instead of the ballroom?"

"I believe it's a very real possibility, Araminta. Nina is dead, yet no one saw her killer either arrive or leave from the ballroom, but the murder weapon was found in Daphne's station, which is in the ballroom right next to the French doors leading to the garden."

"Meeooow!"

Arun burst through the greenery mere inches from Araminta's feet then danced along the row of bushes, turning his head to look back at her and Jacob as if waiting for them to follow.

Jacob's brows rose, and he held out his arm for Araminta to take. "Come along, Minta. We might as well see what he's up to."

A few feet along the hedgerow, a path through the roses broke into view, at which point Sasha's head poked out.

"Meow!"

Araminta drew up. "Oh my, Jacob, would you look at that? It looks like someone has pushed their way through the roses."

Jacob nodded. "Apparently, and in a path that goes directly from the ballroom to the library."

It wasn't really a path per se; it was more of a disturbance. Someone had pushed through the roses, crushing flowers and breaking stems.

"I would say *that* is how the rose petals came to be in the library, Araminta," Jacob pointed out. "No lover's quarrel took place the morning of Nina's murder. I opine the petals in the library were merely a few that decided to catch a ride on our killer when he came through the bushes from the ballroom. He tracked them in."

"Or *she*," Araminta said. She quickly relayed the information she and Trinity had gleaned from Stephen Roy—that he'd seen *Millicent* by the French doors, and he'd even suggested she might have been the killer's accomplice. Perhaps she was Nina's killer?

Jacob took in the new information but held his silence. Araminta, too, was quiet for a moment while deliberating the new details. After a moment, she struck upon a thought that made sense. "Jacob... perhaps the killer wasn't trying to frame Daphne at all, but rather, she was incriminated as a matter of convenience. After all, we were wrong about the roses. We could be wrong about that too."

"What exactly are you suggesting, m'dear?"

"Only that it makes more sense now that we've found the path through the roses to imagine the killer merely stuffed the leash into Daphne's station because hers was closest to the French doors rather than to draw attention to her."

Jacob considered her reasoning.

"Daphne told Ivan and the others she was in the bathroom during the time when Nina would have been murdered. I know it sounds convenient, but with her gone from her station, the killer could easily have slipped in through the French doors and hidden the leash in the first place they saw—in with Daphne's things."

Araminta knew she was on to something, but Jacob seemed to be more interested in her eyes than what her lips were saying. Feeling a bit frustrated by his unusual inattention, she patiently explained, "Everyone was busy with their cats, and the rosebushes would have hidden the killer from view most of the way, so it's conceivable no one would notice the killer slip inside those doors."

"Of course. In through the doors with it, then bury it straight into Daphne's things." Jacob blinked. "It's a possibility."

He stared at Araminta for a moment with something akin to appreciation in his eyes. "You're getting better at figuring these things out, Araminta. Much, much better," he said, as he patted the top of her hand, which still lay comfortably on the strength of his arm. Her eyes narrowed, but he merely smiled at her and winked. "Yes, m'dear, I think I'd be remiss in giving you your due if I didn't at least admit you're almost as good as me."

"*Almost* as good? Are you saying at this moment, you somehow know more about Nina's killer than I do, Jacob Hershey?" Araminta removed her hand from his arm and headed for one of the intricate wrought iron and stone benches on the patio outside the library. "Come then, shall we? Let us review *the clues.*"

Following slightly behind her, Jacob laughed. "Finally, the voice of reason. I'll have Harold speak with Mary about bringing us a light snack, if you don't mind? I've a taste for some of those delightful finger sandwiches she makes and perhaps a spot of tea."

# CHAPTER SIXTEEN

Trinity busied herself with setting out plates while Araminta and Jacob bantered back and forth about Bertie's arrival before getting down to the specifics of the case. Araminta was happy to see Bertie, while Jacob seemed disgruntled by his being there. They talked for a few minutes about how terrible it was, this awful thing had happened to their friend Daphne, and how they had to save her.

Then—and Trinity had to hide a smile this time—the conversation turned to a grumbled suggestion or two that something might be going on between "that niece of yours," who was Stephanie, and "that far too serious grandson of yours," who was obviously Ivan.

After she'd placed the finger sandwiches Jacob had requested on the table and given both Araminta and Jacob a light salad that Mary had sent out along with slices of fresh-made bread and cheese and crackers, Trinity hurried back inside.

Jacob poked at his salad with his fork. His brows were drawn close, and he had fallen silent.

"You're harried, Jacob. You've got that look about you," Araminta pointed out when he started to protest.

He relaxed and offered a bit of a smile. "You know me too well, Minta. Back when I was on the force, I used to go off alone for a day or two at this point. There was always a blur of sorts—that moment when statements and body language and clues all tend to meld together into one big, gray mass of subterfuge and confusion."

Araminta broke off three tiny pieces of cheese and slipped them under the table to Arun, Sasha, and Codger, who had been sitting there patiently, waiting.

She remembered those days when they were young and Jacob was on the force. And she knew exactly how to break Jacob out of his current gray fog. "Well, then. We have arrived at last, it seems, and we both know there is but one thing left to do: we must reexamine *the clues*."

Jacob took a bite of his salad, but he was staring off into the gardens, distracted still. "The book bothers me, Minta."

"Mew!" Arun batted at Araminta's toe, presumably wanting another piece of cheese.

"The one about the cat breeds?"

"Yes, that one." He tilted his head, considering. "No one can tell us whether Nina was reading it or using it to defend herself, but from the way it was lying beside her on the floor, it must have fallen during the struggle."

Araminta nodded. "I haven't heard a word from anyone about the book, but it surely figures in somewhere. I suppose she must have been reading it. My question is why? Nina clearly knew breeds. What would she have been looking for? And why would it have mattered to whoever ended her life?"

Jacob shook his head and picked up a sandwich. "More questions than answers there, for certain."

"One question has been answered, though Ivan and his boys missed it initially. That one was a good catch, Jacob. I have to admit I probably would have missed it."

Jacob's eyes sparkled at the compliment, but he arched a brow in question.

"The brown smudge in the sink. It must be hair dye, and I imagine that Donald is responsible. I'm not sure why he would be doing that in the bathroom, but with Nina here…" She let him draw his own conclusions.

"We also now know the rose petals were most likely accidentally carried in from the garden by whoever came here to the library from the ballroom," she reminded him, moving on to the next physical clue the police had found.

"Yes, which rules out seduction or an affair gone bad being the reason for the murder… or so it seems."

Araminta took a sip of her lemonade. "Yes. Well, actually, no. Not quite. I haven't entirely ruled it out, but it does appear unimportant at this point. Still, if we say the roses were indeed brought in accidentally rather than on purpose, the next question becomes 'by whom?'"

"Don't forget the most important clue. The leash," Jacob reminded her. "It is the murder weapon, after all."

"Meow!" Now it was Sasha's turn to request more cheese. Araminta would have to be careful not to give them too much.

The leash certainly was an interesting clue. All the cat owners had several each, and no one claimed to be missing one. Therefore, it must have been the killer's leash. She told Jacob as much.

He nodded. "Precisely. But this one had a flaw, if you'll recall."

"The smudge," Araminta said. "Of course I remember, Jacob. I would presume it to be blood from the killer getting scratched on the rose thorns, but if it were, wouldn't the police be coming to see who matches the blood type? Unless, of course, it *was* Daphne's blood…"

She injected the slightest hint of disappointment into her tone, but he didn't answer. Instead, he nodded toward the library door.

Araminta turned, following his gaze. "Bertie!"

She waved him forward. "We were just having a late lunch. Join us. I'm sure Jacob won't mind. Would you, Jacob?"

"Of course not," he said. His tone was welcoming, but his expression had gone back to scowling. Under his breath, he muttered to Araminta, "Might as well, since you've invited him over already, and you always get your way."

"Be nice, Jacob. He's a friend." To Bertie, she said, "Sit here, darling, and have a plate. The sandwiches are delicious. Have you had one? Where is Stella?"

"Stella is in the kitchen with Mary," Bertie said as he took a seat.

Trinity came out the double doors from the library with another salad plate in her hand along with an extra plate of bread and cheese.

"Mary thought you might want more," she explained, "What with how Mr. Jacob was praising the sandwiches and all."

Trinity put the plates down then left.

"Mary is very thoughtful," Araminta said.

For the next half hour, Araminta and Jacob were enthralled by Bertie's jewelry stories. He'd been all over the world, it seemed, acquiring the best jewels for his customers. In every port of call, a new acquaintance was made, and thus, a new, wonderful story of adventure was born.

The cats napped in the sun, and Araminta listened with avid interest while Jacob did his best to top each new tale with a "back in my police detective days" story of his own.

"What do you think of the cheddar?" Arun asked as he delicately licked the piece of cheese Araminta had given him.

"It's okay, but I like Camembert the best. I wish they would throw some of that Gouda down," Codger said.

"At least the humans finally caught on to the getaway path of the killer." Sasha stretched out in a patch of sun.

"Took them long enough," Arun said.

"And the stain in the bathroom," Codger added. "Though I must admit that one has me a bit baffled."

"Don't worry. Araminta will figure it out." Sasha was proud of her human's skills of deduction.

"Umm… I think it will be Jacob who deduces the identity of the killer," Codger said, sounding every bit as smug as his human did sometimes.

Arun batted at an acorn, sending it skittering across the brick walkway. "Araminta usually figures it out."

Codger shook his head. "Nope, Jacob does. He's trained."

Arun stared at him. "Is that what Jacob tells you? Because over here, we get a different story."

Codger stretched out and then curled into a ball in the sun. "Well, that makes sense. Each human tells the story that makes them look the best."

Arun preened his whiskers. "I suppose. Speaking of stories, these ones that Bertie and Jacob are telling are a bit boring."

"No kidding," Sasha agreed. "What do you make of Bertie?"

Codger slitted one eye open and looked up at the old man. "He's not as handsome as Jacob. I don't know what Araminta sees in him."

"They're just old friends, Codger. But the assistant, Stella. I'm not too sure about her."

"Why do you say that?" Arun asked.

"It's just that she is very young. He is very old, and they seem very close." Sasha licked a velvety brown paw and then wiped behind her ears.

Arun shook his head. "Eh, humans. Who can ever understand them?"

All three cats swished their tails in agreement.

"Right now, though, Bertie and his assistant are not our concern." Sasha's blue eyes turned darkly serious. "There is a killer on the loose, and we have to help our humans figure out who it is."

"And for that," Arun added as he curled into a ball, tucking his nose under his tail, "we need catnaps. We'll think much better with rested brains."

Though the spirit of the contest had been dampened by Nina's murder, there was still a cat show to judge. After her snack with Jacob and Bertie, Araminta joined both contestants and spectators in the Moorecliff ballroom for the agility round.

Daisy stood with Araminta, watching each cat go through various tests of their skill, a smile on her lips most of the time. First was Jasmine. As Millicent cajoled, ordered, and tugged Jasmine through her round, Daisy whispered to Araminta.

"I visited Daphne. Bless her, she is trying so hard to keep her chin high, but she is quite distraught, Araminta. Are you and Jacob any closer to figuring out who did this?"

"Jacob, of course, is going over every clue with a fine-tooth comb. He's found few answers. Far more questions, actually."

"And you?" she asked then clapped when Jasmine

actually cleared a hurdle. "Have you found anything that will free Daphne from her unfair incarceration?"

Araminta sighed. "I wish I could say yes, Daisy, but you understand these things take time. The answers do not show themselves immediately. I've talked to every one of the contestants, and each has revealed something that was previously unknown…"

"Oh?" Daisy gave her a curious glance then hid a chuckle when Loughley, Clint Sterling's cat, sat down when he was supposed to run. Rather than move through the obstacle course, he was more content to groom himself. "What have you learned from the contestants?"

"Most surprising was that Mr. Roy has taken over the underground crime scene as the new boss. Trinity verified that with Viv. Other than that, I know Mr. Copperfield was having an affair with Ms. Bellaforte, the killer traveled from the ballroom to the library and back through the rose garden, and someone made a mess in the bathroom sink."

Daisy winced. "There's not much to go on, is there?"

Araminta shook her head. "There rarely is, Daisy, and yet we've figured out the killer behind three murders recently. I don't know about Jacob, but I certainly am not planning to allow this one to be the one I failed."

Daisy clapped loudly for Bjorn as he maneuvered through the agility portion of the contest without a hitch. "I believe you will figure it out, Araminta. You know I have every faith in your ability. I just hope you can figure it out before the show ends. Tomorrow is the final judging, and then everyone leaves."

Araminta decided to focus on the show and let her subconscious work on the murder. The announcer had just given Bjorn, Stephen Roy's cat, the round, and she was genuinely happy for the feline. Clearly, the Norwegian took his tasks seriously. Leaning toward Daisy, she mentioned that Stephen's cat was very good. Then she said, "And so am I, Daisy. I will figure out who framed Daphne for Ms. Bellaforte's murder."

Daisy gave her a hug. "Thank you, Araminta. I knew we could count on you."

As the contestants' owners crated their cats and retired from the ballroom for the evening, Araminta watched them all with a careful eye. Daisy was right. Tomorrow was the final contest. She had less than twenty-four hours to figure out the identity of Nina's murderer or risk letting a killer go free.

If she didn't solve this puzzle soon, her longtime friend was doomed to spend the rest of her life in jail for a crime Araminta knew Daphne did not have the will nor the heart to commit. Araminta knew there was only one acceptable course of action: free Daphne. Her only problem was figuring out how. She and Jacob had gone over every clue already and found nothing new.

Every direction she had considered thus far had been wrong. Millicent, Donald, Stephen, Clint... each one seemed to be perfectly innocent. There was only one angle left to consider, and it was one Araminta one hundred percent refused to concede.

Was it possible Daphne was Nina's murderer after all? Araminta was as certain as she was bold that the answer to that question was an unequivocal no, but the clues she and Jacob had discussed—the leash was found in Daphne's station, after all—only pointed to her. But if Daphne *had* killed Nina, why had she done so? What would have been her reason?

# CHAPTER EIGHTEEN

$\mathcal{D}$inner provided no further clues, and Araminta was a bit downtrodden as she retired to her chamber for the evening.

Shaggy was sitting in the window seat, staring out at the night. When she entered, he turned his sad cat eyes on her. Araminta picked him up and cradled him in her arms.

"Don't worry. I will find out who did this, and you will soon be back with Daphne."

As always, it came down to motive, and Araminta knew she must consider each suspect more closely.

Pacing her chamber, with Arun, Sasha, and Shaggy following along beside her, Araminta considered each contestant and the most obvious motive: money. Money was always a deciding factor in tragedies like this one, she knew, and that was why she didn't believe Daphne was guilty. She wouldn't have needed the prize money at all, and in fact, she did not. She'd only entered

Shaggy in the cat show because Jacob had suggested she do so as a way for the two of them to spend time with Araminta while she was here. But even if she had, between herself, Jacob, Daisy, Steph, Reggie, and Bertie, they would all have made sure Daphne was taken care of.

Stephen Roy obviously did not need the money either given his new status as the leader of the city's darker, seedier underbelly. And Clint Sterling? His family came from money. He would only want to win for the prestige—to mollify his father. Donald Copperfield would be the obvious suspect because of the affair, but he had an alibi … which left only Millicent Copperfield, spurned wife of a cheating but very wealthy husband.

Stephen Roy had told her Millicent was seen near the doors by Daphne's station, and Nina had tried to ruin Millicent's cat, Jasmine's, chances in the contest. Did she know Donald and Nina were having an affair?

Maybe Millicent knew all about what was going on between Ms. Bellaforte and her husband. Maybe she knew Nina was trying to get Donald to leave her, and she didn't want him to take all his money with him. It made sense, and that was why, with all things considered, Millicent seemed the most likely suspect to have murdered Nina.

And, come to think of it, Donald wasn't the only one who dyed his hair. Araminta had seen the inkling of gray roots in Millicent's hair. Was she the one who had done a touch-up in the bathroom? And what of the smudge on the leash? Could it be hair dye from Millicent's touch-up job?

Millicent would have two reasons not to like Nina. One was that she'd put gum in Jasmine's fur. The other was that she was cheating with her husband. Would that be enough reason to kill? Perhaps.

But Araminta had another clue that might reveal the identity of the killer. The rosebushes the killer had used to travel from the ballroom to the library and back again were full of thorns. Surely the killer must have some scratches from that.

All Araminta had to do to prove it was Millicent was visit with her the next morning and get her to roll up her sleeves somehow to reveal the scratches. Satisfied with her plan, Araminta tucked the cats into their cushioned cat beds, put on her pajamas, and settled in for the night.

# CHAPTER NINETEEN

After a troubled, fitful sleep filled with horrible nightmares wherein Daphne accused her of letting the real killer go free and Jacob shunned her for refusing to follow the clues to the truth of who framed their friend, Araminta rose early on the final day of the annual Moorecliff Manor Cat Show.

Feeling the need for an extra boost of confidence today of all days, she chose her smartest outfit for the judging of the contest... and for confronting Millicent Copperfield about her crime—a lime-green, high-necked button-up blouse with bright-yellow peplums over a pair of brilliant peacock-blue slacks.

On her head, she perched a matching peacock-blue hat with lime feathers and yellow streamers. The cats seemed quite fascinated with the streamers, and Araminta almost had to choose another one, but once she stood, the streamers were no longer in reach of the cats. She'd have to be careful when she was sitting, though.

The little darlings couldn't resist batting at the dangling embellishments and had no qualms about jumping in the air to do so.

Her shoes were chosen for comfort—a pair of bright-yellow pumps with navy-blue faux pearls and lime-green ribbons over the toes for accent. She also chose a fine peridot necklace, yellow citrine-and-diamond earrings, and a sapphire-and-pearl bracelet just to complement the outfit.

After a quick, minimal dash of makeup, Araminta gave herself a final check in her mirror then patted the peplums above her hips, called to her kitties, and decisively left the room. She was ready. This murder mystery had gone on long enough. It was time to confront a killer.

The first blow to her confidence came the moment she stepped into the ballroom. Millicent was already there, tending to Jasmine's needs before today's final reveal.

Her food and water bowl had been filled, but Araminta didn't pay attention to either because she was stumped yet again. Millicent was wearing a sleeveless dress, and there wasn't a single scratch visible on her bare hands and arms. How could she have possibly gone through the rosebushes without a single scratch?

As she approached, Millicent blinked, fanned her face, then gave a short laugh. "You suddenly look deflated, Ms. Moorecliff. Is everything all right? Beautiful outfit, by the way."

Araminta pushed her palms down the hem of her

blouse again. She could feel the tension in her brow and could well imagine the expression she must have presented to Millicent on her approach. "I—ah—have a confession to make, actually."

Millicent looked up from her careful brushing of Jasmine's fur. "Oh? Do tell."

Araminta took a deep breath. "Mrs. Copperfield… ah, Millicent, I hate to bring it up, but in light of the circumstances with Ms. Bellaforte and all—did you know? What I mean is, were you aware that your husband was having an affair with her?"

After a moment, Millicent nodded. "I did. Do you think my husband killed her?"

Araminta hid a grimace. "Actually, when I came down this morning, I was convinced you were the one who was guilty of murder. But then I saw your dress."

Millicent looked confused. "My dress? I don't understand."

"The sleeves, or rather, the lack thereof. You see, whoever killed Nina would be covered with scratches. From the rosebushes. Have you seen any cuts or scratches on your husband, Mrs. Copperfield?"

Millicent shook her head. "I have not. But why were you certain I murdered Miss Bellaforte?"

"Because your husband is wealthy, and Ms. Bellaforte's niece told me Nina was trying to convince Donald to leave you. I was certain money was your motive. You obviously enjoy an expensive lifestyle, but with Donald gone, how would you support yourself?"

At that, Millicent laughed. "I have grown used to

Donald's affairs over the years, but even if I hadn't, I would never kill him for leaving me and most especially not for his money. You see, Donald doesn't have any. The Copperfield money is mine."

It was Araminta's turn to be surprised. "Now, there's a tidbit you don't learn unless you ask, I suppose."

"Perhaps." Millicent bent her head to focus on fluffing Jasmine's tail, and Araminta noticed she still had the gray roots. Millicent hadn't touched them up in the sink. So then, who had?

Araminta glanced around the ballroom at her suspects. Stephen Roy and Clint Sterling both had distinguished grays creeping in. Daphne, of course, colored hers, and then she was back to Donald. He'd claimed to be in a board meeting, but could he have coerced the other people to lie for him? Araminta assumed the police had checked his alibi, but she actually didn't even know if Donald was on their radar as a suspect.

"I was wondering, did Donald dye his hair in the bathroom sink down here?" Even as Araminta asked the question, she realized it was silly. Why wouldn't he just go upstairs to their private suite?

Millicent must have been thinking the same. "Here? I should say not. He does that at home. Makes a big mess too."

"Right. That makes sense."

Millicent suddenly cleared her throat. Araminta glanced at her, and she made a motion with her head toward the other end of the room. Donald was heading their way. Recognizing Millicent's signal for what it was —heads-up that her husband was approaching and they should wrap up the present conversation—Araminta said, "Thank you for your time, Mrs. Copperfield. Good luck with Jasmine and the judges this afternoon."

# CHAPTER TWENTY

Araminta spotted Jacob and hurried over to fill him in on her chat with Millicent. "I suppose you were right, Jacob. I shouldn't follow my gut or hunches or wild ideas not supported by the clues—the actual, factual evidence. The only thing I've accomplished by my insistence to question Millicent is making myself look ridiculous."

Jacob gave her a once-over, his eyes twinkling. "You look splendid, Minta. Positively adorable. Did I buy you that hat? It seems very familiar now that I'm seeing it up close."

Araminta blushed. "You did, and if you truly don't remember, I'll be surprised. It was the Donemonde case, remember? He was a famous hatter on the East End. When you handed him over to the police, you put the money for it on the counter and told him you were going to be his last customer ever."

"Donemonde. Oh, yes, I remember that one well. He was enchanted by you—even though you made an absolute cake of yourself, pretending to be falling for him."

Araminta gave him a look. "Who says I was pretending? He was quite the rogue, you know."

Jacob laughed. "So were you if I remember correctly."

Whether he did or not, Araminta certainly did. She had played the gambler in that case—a good luck charm for a player dealing in rare jewels. "Bertie was fabulous, wasn't he?"

Jacob scowled. "Let's not talk about him, Araminta. He has a terrible habit of showing up every time his name is mentioned, and I'd rather discuss the clues before we are interrupted. There is one that I feel is most important—the book."

Araminta sharply reined in her thoughts and nodded. "Of course. What have you discovered?"

"Nothing, and that is what puzzles me," he admitted —a rare thing for Jacob. "There must be a reason the book was there, Araminta, but we haven't a single angle to pursue that leads to that reason."

"I've spoken with all the contestants, and no one has said a word about it. Each of them are well versed in breeds. Nina knew as well. I have to confess, I am as stumped as you—but we have to do something, Jacob. Daphne needs us."

He nodded. "Of course she does. We both know she

isn't guilty. We simply have to find enough proof to convince Ivan of it."

"I could speak to Stephanie," Araminta offered.

Jacob shook his head. "The boy is addled enough by her as it is, Minta. Feels like he's off his game, and quite frankly, he's embarrassed to have been the one to take Daphne in. He's known her forever—she's like the great-aunt he never had, and yet he was forced to arrest her."

Araminta could well understand the young man's reticence. "Can we not argue that the location of the leash is merely circumstantial?"

"We can," Jacob told her. "The minute we have proof of why."

Once again, Araminta felt her spirits fall. Daphne was going to spend the rest of her life in a cell because her best friends in all the world had failed her. Looking up at Jacob with watery eyes, she asked, "How?"

Jacob put his finger under her chin and tilted it up before he reached up to run a finger along the rim of her hat. "I don't know, Araminta, but there is one thing I do know."

"What is that, Jacob Hershey? That I've failed because I refuse to look at only the facts? The clues?" She could feel her eyes filling but refused to allow a tear to fall. No, she was not the type of woman to cry when things seemed out of her reach. She was the kind who ignored it all and barreled forward until she found a way to have what she wanted.

"No," Jacob told her. "I know with absolute certainty you will figure this out, Araminta. Not because you've followed the clues, or you've interrogated everyone involved, but because you're the most determined woman I know. No matter how dim or dire the circumstances, you always find the answers you're looking for. You're the best partner in crime a man could ever wish for."

"You mean that, Jacob Hershey?" she asked with a little sniff.

He chucked her under the chin and smiled. "Every word… even under oath."

Araminta laughed. "Well then, I suppose I should get busy finding our killer. I would hate to see you perjure yourself for little old me."

While they were talking, Sasha and Arun had wandered across the ballroom to Loughley's crate and were even now scratching and meowing at the box. It was empty because Clint Sterling had come in a few minutes ago and taken the striking Bengal cat outside to the gazebo for his morning walk.

"Oh dear," Araminta said. "Those two are always up to something."

Jacob turned his head to watch the pair cavorting around the crate.

"I'm surprised Codger isn't up to something with them. But then, I suppose he's taking care of things in his own way," he told her then nodded toward the door leading to the garden. Across the way, Araminta could see Codger just outside the library, sitting casually on the stone wall. His tail twitched once, and he turned and tipped up his chin as if to signal to Jacob that he had something to tell him.

Araminta laughed again. "You'd better go see what he's found while I check in with these two."

"She's coming over!" Sasha pranced in front of Loughley's crate, her tail in the air.

"About time." Arun trotted over to Araminta to lead her the rest of the way, just in case she got sidetracked.

"How do we get her to look inside?" Sasha asked as he trotted away.

"I'm sure you can figure it out," Arun shot over his shoulder.

Sasha flicked her tail at him. He could be a bit condescending at times. Well, she would show him!

Araminta arrived at the crate, and Sasha rubbed her cheek on the side and meowed, looking up at Araminta with the cutest kitten face she could muster.

Araminta bent to scoop Sasha up in her arms without giving the crate a glance. "What are you two doing over here?"

"Meow!" Sasha wiggled in her arms.

"Guess that didn't work." Arun stretched and poked his nose at the carrier.

"Come now, you two. The show will be starting as soon as breakfast is over. We should go see Mary for our own."

Patting her thigh, Araminta gestured for Arun to

come to her. "We can walk in the kitchen garden after. With Codger. And I'm sure Jacob and Bertie will be there."

Sasha twisted and jumped down. She strutted back and forth in front of Loughley's crate. Araminta frowned. Sasha could tell by the look of interest in her eye that she was getting the message. Phew!

Araminta looked around, presumably to make sure Mr. Sterling wasn't nearby, then she bent down to examine the crate. She opened the door and pulled out a clump of cat fur.

"Meow!" Sasha tried to encourage her.

"It is sad, I know," she told Sasha. "I think Mr. Sterling is a decent owner, but Loughley is clearly stressed. Why else would he be shedding?"

Standing, Araminta patted her thighs yet again.

"Come on. It's time for us to leave while the groomers work. Unless you'd like to be groomed by one of them yourselves," she threatened, thinking that would set them into motion. Neither Sasha nor Arun enjoyed their sessions with the groomers in town.

"Darn it! She was almost there," Sasha said.

"I know how to get her to pay more attention." Araminta had left the crate door open, and Arun nudged it wider then slipped inside and plopped down, swishing his tail back and forth, stirring up more clumps of fur.

"Arun, you naughty boy, get out of there!" Araminta gestured for Arun to follow her, but he stayed inside the crate.

Araminta sighed and reached to scoop him out.

When she did, a poof of hair stuck to her bright-lime sleeve.

"Cat hair!" Araminta deposited Arun on the floor and locked the door to the crate. "Luckily, I'm used to removing the hair with you two."

Araminta proceeded to brush the hairs off, but then she stopped. She held up one hair, dark black from tip to root.

"Oh, now wait a minute here." Araminta's head snapped up, and she scanned the room, probably looking for Jacob, Arun surmised.

"There," Arun told Sasha. "She's figured it out."

And indeed, Araminta did know what happened. She knew who murdered Nina Bellaforte, and she knew why. Jacob had been right about the book being important.

"You two are brilliant! Thank you both so much!" Araminta scooped Sasha up and gave both her and Arun a big cuddle before putting them both back on the floor.

"You *two*?" Arun complained. "Why do you get the credit too? I was the one that led her to the solution."

"Go to Mary," Araminta told them. "I will be along directly."

"Because we both helped her figure it out, you big ball of fur," Sasha told him while they walked together, as a pair, toward the door.

"Whatever," Arun said, though he had stopped to

watch Araminta hurry across the room toward the French doors. "Let's find Mary. I'm starving."

The cats loped out of the ballroom on one side, and Araminta left almost at a run through the other. She had one last thing to verify, and she'd better be quick about it.

# CHAPTER TWENTY-ONE

From his seat in the crowd, Jacob watched the contestants show off for the guests while their owners waited for the final judging of the contest and the awarding of the grand prize. Which one, he wondered, would commit murder to take the prize?

Money was usually a powerful motivator for murder. Like Araminta, he knew this was their last chance to find Nina's killer. As he watched her speaking to Harold on the west side of the ballroom, he felt a bit nervous, but only a bit. He hadn't lied to her earlier. He truly believed if anyone could figure out who murdered Nina Bellaforte in the grand Moorecliff Manor, it would be her. He only hoped she would put the pieces together before the contest ended and the crowd dispersed.

For himself, he literally didn't have a clue. Those he did have had been exhausted. The trail, as the phrase went, had gone cold. Poor Daphne. She must be terrified.

Next, the judges walked on stage, and the crowd quieted. It was time. Casting one last glance at Araminta, he saw her make her way across the ballroom toward the stage.

"Welcome, welcome!" the speaker for the judges said into the microphone. "Thank you for being here to support the fifth annual Moorecliff Manor Cat Show!"

Everyone clapped, then the speaker continued by listing this year's contestants: Jasmine, Bjorn, and Loughley. No one mentioned the fact that Zsa Zsa and Shaggy had been disqualified because someone was murdered.

"Before we announce this year's winner of the twenty-five-thousand-dollar grand prize, we would like to take a moment to thank our sponsors, and none more so than the lady responsible for organizing and hosting our event, Araminta Moorecliff!"

Araminta smiled and waved to the crowd as she made her way onto the stage to say a few words about the competition. From the corner of his eye, Jacob saw Ivan come in with Stephanie and take a seat in the crowd. A couple of uniformed police officers had come with him, hanging toward the back. Jacob nodded an acknowledgment to his grandson then turned his attention back to Araminta.

"Thank you all for being here," she started. "As you know, the annual Moorecliff Cat Show seeks to honor the best of the best feline breeds, and this year, I am pleased for us to be introduced to not only a beautiful lady Persian and a strong Norwegian Forest cat, we also had the pleasure of meeting our first Bengal."

Jacob felt his brows draw together. Why was she talking about the breeds? Shouldn't she be thanking the guests and contestants? Curious, he folded his arms across his chest and settled back in his chair, interested to see how her speech would unfold.

"As I had never been around Bengals before Mr. Sterling's entry this year, I did a bit of research into the breed. I'm sure most of you are already aware, but for those who aren't, Bengal cats are a hybrid breed that were perfected in the 1980s by Jean Sugden Mill. This particular breed loves to learn tricks and to perform. Mr. Sterling could not have chosen a better breed to present—I am sure his father must be very proud."

Jacob, like most of the crowd, turned his attention to Clint Sterling and the feline he'd entered into this year's contest. Loughley lounged on his table while Mr. Sterling, who was seated behind the table, appeared to be uneasy with the attention focused on him.

"Bengals generally have striking leopard-like markings, and naturally, as part of the judging, the markings must be to breed standard, as it is with all breeds." Araminta leveled her gaze at Clint Sterling, who squirmed in his seat.

Jacob felt the rush of excitement that comes when a case gets solved. Araminta was onto something. He leaned forward in his seat as she continued.

"With the Bengal breed, it is those gorgeous ringed

black-and-brown spots. But if the spots are not formed to the breed standard, then naturally, the cat will lose points in the judging." Araminta gestured toward Loughley. "And if the spots have been doctored, well then, the cat would be disqualified entirely."

Gasps were heard throughout the crowd. Jacob blinked. The judges immediately began to whisper to each other.

"Well, I'll be darned," Jacob whispered to himself. She had figured it out.

Turning to the judges, Araminta said, "Unfortunately, Clint Sterling has done just that with Loughley. If you examine the cat, you will find that Clint has dyed the hair to cover up the fact that the cat's markings are, indeed, imperfect."

As he watched, Araminta pinned Clint Sterling with a look that must have rendered him immobile because he stopped fidgeting with his coat and now sat stock-still while he and the crowd waited for Araminta to finish.

Araminta continued, "Nina must have figured it out. Maybe she'd seen him take Loughley into the bathroom that morning to touch up the dye. It certainly would be unusual to take one's cat in there… and that was why she was reading a book about cat breeds in the library. She wasn't looking for information on *breeds*— she was looking up their *markings*. When he saw her reading it in the library, that book became the precise tell that made her killer realize she was onto him."

Araminta turned slightly to find him in the crowd,

and her chin tipped upward. The gesture was mostly imperceptible, but Jacob saw it. She was giving him a nod to acknowledge he'd been right about the book being important.

"Poor Nina," she continued. "It saddens me that her Zsa Zsa, along with our good friend Ms. Burgess's cat, Shaggy, had to be disqualified. But that is being handled by our good friends down at the station, so let us move along."

She motioned to Clint Sterling's station. "I'm not sure how Nina figured it out. I suppose we'll never know. She wasn't one to hold her tongue. Did she confront you, Mr. Sterling?"

"This is outrageous!" Clint Sterling stood, but the two uniformed officers who were now standing behind his chair pushed him back down.

"We'll leave that for the police to find out. Either way, Clint tracked her down in the library. He must have brought Loughley's leash. Did you get a smudge of hair dye on the leash, Mr. Sterling?" Araminta didn't wait for him to answer. "I'm not sure if he intended to kill her. Maybe he just wanted to ensure her silence, and when she didn't grant that silence, he strangled her."

The crowd gasped, and several people sitting near Sterling scooted their chairs away.

"Preposterous!" Sterling yelled. "She's crazy. I'll sue!"

Araminta shook her head at Sterling. "No, I am not crazy. The clues are all there. For example, I have deduced that the killer traveled between the ballroom and the library through the rosebushes in the atrium. Daphne's station is just inside the French doors, where you found a convenient place to stash the murder weapon."

"You can't prove—" Sterling's outraged cry was shushed by the crowd.

Peering at Clint, Araminta's gaze narrowed. Lifting her hand, she motioned to Ivan then said, "Mr. Sterling, would you please remove your gloves and roll up your sleeves?"

With the lead detective from the case headed in his direction and two police officers standing behind him, Clint Sterling slowly did as he'd been asked. The crowd gasped again when Clint removed his gloves. They could clearly see the crisscrossed scratches on his hands and arms from the rosebushes.

Ivan put the cuffs on Clint Sterling himself, and the crowd exploded into chaos. Araminta lifted her hand toward the audience, gesturing for quiet as she spoke to the police detective. "Mr. Hershey? Could you please do us the honor of taking Mr. Sterling from the ballroom? I would be very appreciative if you would also have your man make a call to the station to let Ms. Daphne Burgess know she is free to leave."

In his seat, Jacob could barely contain either his excitement or his pride. She'd done it!

Somehow, with a cold trail of clues and confusing confessions from their suspects, Araminta had figured out who murdered Nina Bellaforte. Not only had she solved the crime, she had revealed it to all in a way he would never have considered, but in all the years he'd known her, no one handled solving a crime with the same level of class, flair, and style like Araminta Moorecliff.

# CHAPTER TWENTY-TWO

Due to the fact that the contestant's owner was a murderer, Clint and Loughley were disqualified from the contest. The fifth annual Moorecliff Manor Cat Show award went instead to Bjorn, the Norwegian Forest cat that belonged to a man Araminta now knew was the leader of a local crime ring.

Not that she could tell the judges who had awarded the prize to him. She had no proof—only hearsay. Or was it a confession?

Whatever the manner of Mr. Roy's unsavory profession, he managed to surprise Araminta and the crowd at Moorecliff Manor when he accepted the win—he thanked everyone very prettily then turned around and gifted the entire twenty-five thousand dollars of prize money to Daphne, saying that he understood her plight and that he would personally hate to be unfairly accused of a crime he didn't commit.

Given that Daphne was forced to miss the contest

altogether through no fault of her own and the damage to her reputation due to being falsely accused, he thought the prize should go to her.

Daphne, too, was stunned by Mr. Roy's generosity, and she told everyone so the moment she was reunited with Jacob, Araminta, and Bertie at Moorecliff Manor.

They were having a bit of a reminisce in the dining room, along with Stephanie and Ivan, and Bertie seemed unable to contain his surprise and delight that Araminta had solved the murder case. Jacob, however, swore he'd had no doubt. Araminta was an extraordinary woman with extraordinary skills.

"How did you figure it out, Ms. Moorecliff?" Stella's eyes were wide as she plucked a grape from the charcuterie board and popped it into her mouth.

Araminta beamed with pride until Jacob cleared his throat rather loudly. "Well, it wasn't *just* me. Jacob helped."

"Helped?" Jacob looked amused.

Araminta grimaced. "More than helped. We're a team, and we figured it out together. You see, we went over all the clues and suspects and then were able to deduce who the killer was before the police."

Now it was Ivan's turn to clear his throat.

"Oh, well, err… I guess Ivan had come to the same conclusion at about the same time." Araminta smiled her thanks at Trinity, who had stepped forward from her spot next to the server to top off her glass of wine.

"Ivan is the best detective." Stephanie looked up at Ivan from under her lashes, causing him to blush.

Araminta took a sip of wine. "I probably could have solved it sooner if I'd only looked at Loughley's hair a bit closer."

"His hair?" Daisy asked.

Araminta gestured toward Arun and Sasha, who were lounging by the fireplace with Codger and Shaggy. "I'm no stranger to cat hair, and as with most animals, the individual hairs are rarely one single color. Arun and Sasha have lovely cream-colored hairs with dark tips. Even their darker hairs have black at the root." Araminta paused to take another sip of wine. All eyes were on her. "But the hair from Loughley's crate was all dark with no variation."

"Of course it took more than that one clue to solve the case," Ivan pointed out.

"Oh yes, of course!" Araminta agreed. "But I should have clued in early on when the cat was shedding so much. You see, the dye irritated his skin. And then there was the fact the killer was wearing long sleeves and gloves. He said it was to keep the fur from getting oily residue that would reduce the natural sheen."

"And the book was a major clue," Jacob said.

"Yes, of course, Jacob. Nina must have noticed something was off about Loughley's fur pattern, and she was looking it up."

"And none of the judges noticed anything odd about the cat's markings?" Stella seemed skeptical.

"All of the judges are volunteers. They aren't well versed in the more exotic breeds, I'm afraid. This is, after all, a small-time cat show and mostly for charity. We can't afford the professional judges." Araminta turned to Daphne, who was seated beside her, and patted her arm. "I'm just glad we have our Daphne back with us."

"Me too," Daphne said. "And thanks to you and Jacob… and Detective Hershey."

"You're very welcome, dear," Jacob said to Daphne. "I will admit that it's been exciting, but I am looking forward to a calmer week without the hustle and bustle of the cat show and investigation and without all the guests."

Araminta thought she saw Jacob give Bertie a pointed look with his last remark.

Daisy raised her glass. "I agree. It's nice to have guests and a big event, but I'll drink to less hectic times at Moorecliff Manor!"

Arun adjusted his position to get more heat from the roaring fire and licked his front paws. The guests had been feeding them scraps under the table, and he had a few crumbs on his fur.

"We didn't get any credit for solving these murders," Arun said after he hoovered up a crumb from a buttery roll.

"At least your human figured things out." Shaggy stared at Araminta with admiration in his golden eyes.

"And mine," Codger said.

"Oh, yes, Jacob too," Shaggy said.

"We helped," Arun added.

"If it wasn't for us and our humans, Ivan might not catch anyone," Codger joked.

"Detective Hershey does seem more interested in making doe eyes at Stephanie," Shaggy said.

"Yech!" Sasha hissed.

"Humans are so strange," Arun added.

"This whole thing is a shame for the disqualified cats, but Bjorn did deserve to win. He was dreamy." Sasha's sigh earned an annoyed look from Arun.

Codger cleared his throat. "I heard Loughley got a good home."

Sasha nodded. "A pretty cat like him wouldn't be hard to rehome. He's going to live with Emily Primble. She already has several cats but will spoil him along with the others."

"And no more irritating hair dye," Codger said.

"Zsa Zsa almost wasn't as lucky, but I heard Araminta on the phone with Muriel Chase. She was worried because it was obvious Muriel wasn't a cat enthusiast. Luckily, Ms. Chase has given Zsa Zsa to her daughter-in-law, who is an absolute cat lover," Arun said.

"Good news all around." Codger yawned. "But I must say this whole affair has been exhausting."

"Yes, very stressful." Shaggy fluffed out his tail. "I'll be glad to get home to my own cat bed."

"Me too," Codger said.

"I'll be glad to go back to our quiet life without all this commotion and other cats," Arun said.

"Me too," Sasha agreed. "Though with the way Jacob and Araminta have formed a truce, we might be seeing more of Codger around here in the future."

Codger huffed. "I should hope not. I'm quite comfortable alone in my little cottage with Jacob."

"Those two only seem to come together to investigate murders. Let's hope one of those doesn't happen anytime soon, and we can all go back to our regular peaceful lives," Sasha said.

"I'll nap to that!"

And with that, the cats curled into their tails and took a nap.

But the cats would not get their wish to go back to their peaceful lives, because just a little while later….

Soon after dinner was finished, Bertie and then Jacob asked to be excused.

Araminta watched them leave then motioned to Harold. "I have the strangest feeling, Harold. A baseless suspicion, I suppose, but it almost seemed like Bertie sent Jacob a secret signal to follow him. Could you check up on them? Discreetly, of course."

Harold nodded and hurried off to see to her request. Barely a quarter of an hour passed before he returned to her side, looking distraught.

He cleared his throat and shuffled his feet until

Araminta waved him forward once again. "Harold, is everything all right?"

He clasped his hands together and slowly turned his head from side to side. "There's been a bit of mayhem in the mudroom, Ms. Moorecliff. I'm afraid you will all need to follow me."

…. Find out what happens next in book 5, *Mayhem in the Mudroom*

*********

Sign up for my newsletter and get my latest releases at the lowest discount price, plus I'll send you a link for a free download of a book in one of my other series:

https://leighanndobbscozymysteries.gr8.com

Join my readers group on Facebook:
https://www.facebook.com/groups/ldobbsreaders

Like my Facebook Author Page:
https://www.facebook.com/leighanndobbsbooks

ALSO BY LEIGHANN DOBBS

**Cozy Mysteries**

**Moorecliff Manor Cat Cozy Mystery Series**

* * *

*Dead in the Dining Room*

*Stabbed in the Solarium*

*Homicide in the Hydrangeas*

*Lifeless in the Library*

*Mayhem in the Mudroom*

-------

***Mystic Notch***

***Cat Cozy Mystery Series***

* * *

* * *

*Ghostly Paws*

*A Spirited Tail*

*A Mew To A Kill*

*Paws and Effect*

*Probable Paws*

*A Whisker of a Doubt*

*Wrong Side of the Claw*

*Claw and Order*

-------

## Juniper Holiday Cozy Mysteries

***

*Halloween Party Murder*

*Thanksgiving Dinner Death*

*Who Slayed The Santas?*

*Masquerade Party Murder*

*My Fatal Valentine*

-------

## Oyster Cove Guesthouse
## Cat Cozy Mystery Series

***

*A Twist in the Tail*

*A Whisker in the Dark*

*A Purrfect Alibi*

-------

## Kate Diamond Mystery Adventures

***

*Hidden Agemda (Book 1)*

*Ancient Hiss Story (Book 2)*

*Heist Society (Book 3)*

-------

**Silver Hollow**

**Paranormal Cozy Mystery Series**

***

*A Spell of Trouble (Book 1)*

*Spell Disaster (Book 2)*

*Nothing to Croak About (Book 3)*

*Cry Wolf (Book 4)*

*Shear Magic (Book 5)*

-------

**Mooseamuck Island**

**Cozy Mystery Series**

* * *

*A Zen For Murder*

*A Crabby Killer*

*A Treacherous Treasure*

-------

**Blackmoore Sisters**

**Cozy Mystery Series**

* * *

*Dead Wrong*

*Dead & Buried*

*Dead Tide*

*Buried Secrets*

*Deadly Intentions*

*A Grave Mistake*

*Spell Found*

*Fatal Fortune*

*Hidden Secrets*

-------

**Lexy Baker**

**Cozy Mystery Series**

* * *

*Killer Cupcakes*

*Dying For Danish*

*Murder, Money and Marzipan*

*3 Bodies and a Biscotti*

*Brownies, Bodies & Bad Guys*

*Bake, Battle & Roll*

*Wedded Blintz*

*Scones, Skulls & Scams*

*Ice Cream Murder*

*Mummified Meringues*

*Brutal Brulee (Novella)*

*No Scone Unturned*

*Cream Puff Killer*

*Never Say Pie*

*Ain't Seen Muffin Yet*

*Assault and Buttercream*

-------

**Lady Katherine Regency Mysteries**

***

*An Invitation to Murder (Book 1)*

*The Baffling Burglaries of Bath (Book 2)*

*Murder at the Ice Ball (Book 3)*

*A Murderous Affair (Book 4)*

*Murder on Charles Street (Book 5)*

-------

**Julia and Nora Marsh 1920s Cozy Mystery**

***

*Murder on a Mississippi Steamboat*

-------

**Hazel Martin Historical Mystery Series**

***

*Murder at Lowry House (book 1)*

*Murder by Misunderstanding (book 2)*

-------

## Sam Mason Mysteries

## (As L. A. Dobbs)

***

*Telling Lies (Book 1)*

*Keeping Secrets (Book 2)*

*Exposing Truths (Book 3)*

*Betraying Trust (Book 4)*

*Killing Dreams (Book 5)*

-------

## More books in the Rockford Security Series:

Cold As Her Heart

A Game of Kill

No One To Trust

No Time To Run

Don't Fear The Truth

Hide From The Past

-------

## Romantic Comedy

***

## Corporate Chaos Series

*In Over Her Head (book 1)*

*Can't Stand the Heat (book 2)*

*What Goes Around Comes Around (book 3)*

*Careful What You Wish For (4)*

*Dish Best Served Cold (5)*

-------

## Contemporary Romance

***

*Reluctant Romance*

-------

## Sweet Romance (Written As Annie Dobbs)

*Firefly Inn Series*

***

Another Chance (Book 1)

Another Wish (Book 2)

-------

*Hometown Hearts Series*

***

*No Getting Over You (Book 1)*

*A Change of Heart (Book 2)*

-------

**Sweet Mountain Billionaires**

***

*Jaded Billionaire (Book 1)*

*A Billion Reasons Not To Fall In Love (Book 2)*

***

**Sweetrock Sweet and Spicy Cowboy Romance**

*Some Like It Hot*

*Too Close For Comfort*

———

**Regency Romance**

* * *

**Scandals and Spies Series:**

*Kissing The Enemy*

*Deceiving the Duke*

*Tempting the Rival*

*Charming the Spy*

*Pursuing the Traitor*

*Captivating the Captain*

**The Unexpected Series:**

*An Unexpected Proposal*

*An Unexpected Passion*

**Dobbs Fancytales:**

Dobbs Fancytales Boxed Set Collection

———

**Western Historical Romance**

***

**Goldwater Creek Mail Order Brides:**

*Faith*

**American Mail Order Brides Series:**

Chevonne: Bride of Oklahoma

————————

**Magical Romance with a Touch of Mystery**

***

*Something Magical*

*Curiously Enchanted*

# ABOUT THE AUTHOR

USA Today best-selling Author, Leighann Dobbs, has had a passion for reading since she was old enough to hold a book, but she didn't put pen to paper until much later in life. After a twenty-year career as a software engineer, with a few side trips into selling antiques and making jewelry, she realized you can't make a living reading books, so she tried her hand at writing them and discovered she had a passion for that, too! She lives in New Hampshire with her husband, Bruce, their trusty Chihuahua mix, Mojo, and beautiful rescue cat, Kitty.

Find out about her latest books by signing up at:
    https://leighanndobbscozymysteries.gr8.com

Connect with Leighann on Facebook
    http://facebook.com/leighanndobbsbooks

This is a work of fiction.

None of it is real. All names, places, and events are products of the author's imagination. Any resemblance to real names, places, or events are purely coincidental, and should not be construed as being real.

LIFELESS IN THE LIBRARY

Copyright © 2022

Leighann Dobbs Publishing

http://www.leighanndobbs.com

All Rights Reserved.

No part of this work may be used or reproduced in any manner, except as allowable under "fair use," without the express written permission of the author.

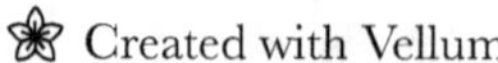 Created with Vellum

www.ingramcontent.com/pod-product-compliance
Lightning Source LLC
Chambersburg PA
CBHW071943190726

48293CB00004B/1314